TEXAS TRIGGER

Bane is a villain — meaner than an outlaw, blood-hungrier than a green cowboy on a spree. He is building his empire in Texas on gunfire and vengeance. Ranger Jim Hatfield takes on the job of stopping Bane. To do this he must penetrate deep into the outlaws' camp — pitting himself against a ruthless, kill-crazy army of evil.

Books by Jackson Cole
in the Linford Western Library:

GUNSLINGER'S RANGE

JACKSON COLE

◆

TEXAS TRIGGER

Complete and Unabridged

LINFORD
Leicester

First published in the
United States of America

First Linford Edition
published September 1992

Copyright © 1946 by Better Publications, Inc.

British Library CIP Data

Cole, Jackson
    Texas trigger.—Large print ed.—
Linford western library
I. Title II. Series
813.52 [F]

ISBN 0–7089–7250–0

Published by
F. A. Thorpe (Publishing) Ltd.
Anstey, Leicestershire

Set by Words & Graphics Ltd.
Anstey, Leicestershire
Printed and bound in Great Britain by
T. J. Press (Padstow) Ltd., Padstow, Cornwall

1

Fresh Blood

THE arrival of the elegant equipage in Culverton caused a stir, drawing the eyes of the loafers on the plaza and the benches in front of Vance Thornton's Elite Hotel & Restaurant. Idle talk, whittling and games of mumblety-peg were suspended as the pair of matched black geldings, their manes laced with red ribbons, curveted to a halt before Thornton's place and the driver jumped down to open the door.

From the patent-leather interior emerged a wiry, quick-moving man in a plain but expensively cut dark suit, fine shined boots and a high-crowned bowler hat.

"Bet yuh four bits he's a sawbones, Mike," said a citizen to a friend.

1

"That's Tom Bailey's best rig from Stafford, and it costs twenty-four dollars a day."

"I can see for myself, Alf," said Mike witheringly. "I ain't en-tirely blind."

"No? Thought yuh might be, the way yuh played that last game!"

The energetic little stranger who had just arrived in town ducked briskly under the rail which served as hitch-rack and at the same time prevented restless mounts from coming up on the sidewalk. The crown of his hat brushed the rail and put it slightly askew. He adjusted it to its proper cant with a hand as he straightened up and stepped up on the porch of the hotel.

After a brief glance around, he went in. He kept the black-leather physician's satchel in his hand, but the driver from Stafford brought in two stuffed carpet-bags.

The sun was large and ruby-red over the Rusty Hills, the wooded slopes to the west of the little Texas Settlement on the winding brown river. The light scintillated blindly on the windows of the adobe and wooden structures leaning amiably toward one another along State Street, Culverton's main thoroughfare.

The plaza was wide, and on its east side were the best stores and saloons, with Thornton's Elite the gathering point for the creme-de-la-creme of town dwellers, ranchers and cowboys off the range, gamblers, bartenders, the town marshal and others of noble callings.

Vast Texas spread to every point of the compass, for hundreds of miles. Far to the west the black-watered Pecos churned through its devious canyons, and the great hinterland of the Lone Star State brooded in the vestiges of the summer day.

There were more interested observers of the new arrival inside the Elite. Some were so intrigued that they crowded about the desk, craning necks and straining eyes to be first to read and announce the inscription the stranger wrote with the quill pen on the register:

Dr. Jno. Bane — New York and London

He did not resent the natural interest of the natives but a faint smile touched his severe, thin lips as he nodded to Vance Thornton, proprietor of the hotel.

"You have a nice town here, sir. I would like the best rooms available, if you please."

"Shore enough, Doc. Got two right together, and Aggie put clean blankets on the bed just this mornin'."

Vance Thornton was a large man whose face was florid from the Texas sun and winds. His thick hair was light, and his wide-set brown eyes good-humored. He wore a blue shirt, open at the neck, and his strong legs were cased in black trousers.

The bar was to the left, while at the other side of the lobby was a connecting door into the restaurant. There were customers in the bar, and more in the restaurant, enjoying an early supper.

Behind a cashier's counter in the restaurant sat a pretty young girl — Della Thornton, the proprietor's daughter. Tight braids of golden hair were pinned neatly about her head. Her brown eyes were wide and her red lips parted as, curious, she watched Dr. Bane's arrival.

Having officiated as clerk, Thornton vaulted the desk.

"Welcome to Culverton, Doc," he said breezily. "I'm mayor, sort of. We hope yuh'll stay with us a while. C'mon, I'll show yuh yore den."

A tall, slender man with graying hair and alert eyes, a man wearing Army blue and a major's insignia, rose from a table in the restaurant and strolled to the doorway. He stood still there, staring, as Dr. Bane, small figure erect and chin up, trailed Vance Thornton to the rear. As they disappeared, the major went to the hotel register and read the inscription which the new guest had written.

It was not long until Thornton returned to his post at the desk. He was smiing.

"He's a good hombre," he announced in his booming voice. "A real fine sawbones. He's come here for his health and he may stick around for a while."

The major, having lighted a cheroot, strolled toward the corridor which have into the rear of the large, rambling Elite.

A fiddle and piano in the bar were tuning up, and soon began playing 'Oh Susannah!' to warm up for the dance. Men had gone back to their drinks, games and gossip. No one noticed the major as he turned the corner in the hall.

Before him was a closed door, with a number on it in black crayon. He rapped on the panel.

"Yes? Bane's voice demanded. "Who is it?"

6

"I'd like to speak to you for a moment, doctor."

The bolt was withdrawn, after a short interval, and Dr. Bane looked out. He had removed his black frock coat, and the bowler hat and bag lay on the table in the middle of the sitting room. Shadows were lengthening and the light was none too good in the corridor, as Bane peered at the major.

"What is it, sir?" asked Bane.

The major pushed in, glancing quickly around. On the floor was a red carpet. There were chairs, oil lamps, and at the windows were lace curtains. Through a door could be seen the bedstead in the other room.

Bane, forced back by the intrusion, turned to face the major. Myriad little lines about his snapping black eyes deepened, and a dark flush spread over his face. The right side of his upper lip and his hawk nose twitched, and a red glow burned in the depths of his eyes.

"I knew it!" the Army officer

exclaimed. "I thought it was you. You've changed in two years, but I'm sure of you. How in blazes did you wriggle out of those charges back in Kansas? You killed that man in cold blood. I thought the Frontier was rid of another quack and faker when they lodged you in jail!" His voice was cold, filled with contempt.

"You — you! You've come here to hound me, I suppose!" Bane's voice was thick with his rising passion.

"No, not at all. Chance brought me here — good fortune for the decent people of the community! I'm just passing through on my way to a new post in Arizona territory. An Army doctor goes where he's ordered. Come with me! I'll turn you over to the authorities here, to make a check-up and see how you managed to escape in Kansas."

The Army medico, a much larger man than Bane, was more than a match for him. Bane raised his voice, begging:

"Please don't give me away! I came

here to start a new life. I give you my word I don't mean any harm."

But the major shrugged. "Your record showed you were dangerous and entirely heartless. You duped the sick and dying unfortunates who came to your door, and when you were exposed you killed in a fit of mad rage. There's nothing to be said for you."

Bane had shifted. The major, turning in order to watch the man he was accusing, had his back to the apparently empty bedroom. But a large man with a fat face and stringy brown hair, appeared silently in the doorway. He leaped at the Army officer from the rear and seized him, a plump arm cutting off the major's cries. A knee to the spine bent the victim back, helpless for a moment, though he tried to wriggle free.

"Quick, Bane, gag him and tie him!" the stout man gasped.

Murderous rage flamed in Bane's black eyes. Gone was the cloak of humility he had assumed, now that his accuser had been tricked. With a snarl he whipped a knife from under his trouser leg. He plunged it into the major, and ripped up, twisting the point as he sought the heart.

Held by the horrified fat man, the officer quivered, and went limp. He sagged, and as the big fellow let go, the major fell lifeless to the rug. With a tigerish lunge, Bane threw himself on the Army man and stabbed again and again, cursing in unsatiated fury.

The stout man, trembling, his teeth chattering in fright, shot the bolt of the door.

"We — better get out, Bane!" he said weakly.

His anger finally abating, Bane got up. He wiped the blood from the knife blade on the major's shirt front. There was a whiteness about his eyes, terrible in their wide staring.

"No, Phelps," he panted. "I don't believe anyone saw the fool come in. He was only passing through, he said. I'm glad he saw me. I've hoped to even

10

up the score with him for what he did in Kansas to convict me. It cost me a fortune to buy out of there. Lucky he wanted to make sure of me before he called the local law."

"But — but you've killed him!" The jowls of the man called Phelps trembled with sickly fear.

Phelps' features were flat, indecisive, his lips thick and wet, and there was nothing spruce about him as there was about Bane. he wore a mussy dark suit, a white shirt with a black string tie, and boots with elastic sides.

He drew a flask from his hip pocket and drank a fortifying draught, then coughed throatily, his washed-out blue eyes filled with tears. Bane was near the door, listening.

"Pull yourself together, Sam," he told Phelps. "We've got to expect this sort of thing now and then. You've done a good job, getting things ready for me, and we won't give up our advantage. I'm going to stay. No one saw you come in, did they?"

"No," Sam Phelps said. "I came through the back, Doc. But I don't like this killin'. Suppose they trace it to you?"

"How can they? The major was only passing through, he told me. No one will miss him for a day or to, and we'll have the body out of here as soon as it's dark tonight . . . Quick, help me move him into the bedroom. Someone's coming down the hall. Be ready in case of trouble. If by any chance we're discovered we'll have to fight for it and run."

They lifted the dead man and took him to the other room, out of sight. Bane tossed a mat over the stain on the red carpet. The music in the salon and the buzz of voices had drowned the sounds of the scuffle.

A sharp rap came on the door and Bane signaled Phelps to hide once more in the bedroom. He replaced his knife, straightened his clothing, and glanced about to be sure all was in order, before he went to open the door.

2

A Story for the Paper

YOUNG Jay Rogers was slightly out of breath as he waited for Dr. Bane's door to open. He had come galloping up the road from the office of the Culverton *Call*, the little weekly belonging to Counselor Samuel Phelps, who had hired Rogers as reporter, assistant printer, associate editor, and whatever else might be necessary to getting out the paper.

Rogers had been hard at work on the editorial which Phelps always signed, when a friend had tipped him off that a famous visitor, a Dr. Bane from abroad and the East, had arrived in the Texas settlement. Such news could not be missed. He would have to make room on the front page, and work into the night, but it would have to be included.

Rogers was a slender, nice-looking young fellow, and his blue eyes were eager with the interest that twenty-two has in unfolding life. He wore an ink-stained shirt and brown trousers, and there were smudges of printer's ink on his face that was browned by the sun and wind. He wore no hat now, and his chestnut hair was damply crisp. He was trying to raise a mustache, because everybody called him 'Son' or 'Bub,' and he desired full adulthood.

He had been a newspaper cub in St. Louis, then had been offered a better job in Austin, the capitol of Texas, as a political reporter. There he had chanced to meet Counselor Samuel Phelps who was planning to start a weekly newspaper in Culverton and had made Rogers an attractive offer to work for him. Rogers would have an important position as editor and chief news gatherer, and so he accepted.

Rogers had a natural aptitude for

newspaper work. He could write well, and he instinctively understood publicity, in which Phelps seemed much interested. Now he was sure he would be pleased if an interview with the new arrival in Culverton was obtained.

The door slowly opened, and before him stood a small but erect figure.

"Are you Dr. Bane?" asked Rogers.

"Yes, yes. What is it?"

"My name's Jay Rogers, Doctor. I'm from the *Call*, our local weekly paper. I'd like an interview, if you have the time. We go to press early in the morning and I need the copy now."

"Very well, come in," invited the doctor. "It's getting dark, isn't it? I'll light the lamp."

The physician was affable. He placed a chair for the reporter with its back to the bedroom door, then struck a match and lighted the lamp on the table. In the yellow glow Rogers mentally noted Bane's appearance — the piercing, dark eyes, the long, slender hands, the surety of manner.

Bane sat down. He picked up a burning cheroot from the tray and puffed at it as he answered Roger's questions.

"Yes, I have practiced in London and New York . . . Specialties? . . . Well, say general surgery and diagnosis. There's little I have not had experience in, as to human ills . . . I like Culverton very much. A fine, growing town with a great future, I'm sure . . . I should like to settle here. Perhaps I will . . . I came here because I must live in a dry climate, and I understand this section has the finest in the Southwest . . . Certainly you may quote me if you wish."

Bane rose and went to one of his bags which he opened.

"Come to think of it, my boy," he said. "I have some newspaper clippings from metropolitan papers which may help you. You may look them over."

Rogers was glad to. They would help fill out his story. The clippings were marked with pencil as to date and

16

source. Some were yellowed. All spoke highly of Dr. Jonathan Bane, surgeon and physician, and Rogers made notes of the best of them.

When his interview was complete. Rogers rose, thanking Dr. Bane.

"I'd say Culverton is lucky to have such a man come to town, Dr. Bane," he said heartily. "I do hope you'll make your home here. I'll see you again, and it was good of you to see me now."

Bane nodded. A smile touched his severe lips. He saw Rogers out, and closed the door . . .

Jay Rogers went through the lobby, looked into the restaurant, and Della Thornton smiled at him. The two young people had become acquainted soon after Rogers' arrival in town. Della always had a smile for Jay as she did now as he went to the cashier's desk to speak to her for a moment before returning to work.

"Hello, Dell," he said. "Busy?"

"Oh, fairly so," she murmured. "Did you talk to the new doctor, Jay?"

"Yes, just got the interview. It'll be in the paper tomorrow. I'll be over later to eat."

"You ought to take your meals regularly, Jay," she said seriously. "It's not good for you, the way you eat."

"I'm all right. Will you be here around nine?"

Dell nodded. "I'll wait for you, if you're sure you won't be running off on a story somewhere, Jay," she said. "Ned asked me to go for a buggy ride, but I can get out of it."

Rogers frowned. He felt a twinge he realized well enough was jealousy of Ned Tenny, a big, good-looking cowboy from the Double A, a ranch a few miles north of town.

"Look for me," he said to Della and left for the newspaper office.

He was hard at work an hour later when Counselor Phelps, his employer and mentor, came into the untidy little office some doors up the way from the Elite. Large and sloppy — lazy, too, Rogers had found — Phelps had political aspirations. And he knew the methods to advance himself.

Tonight Phelps was quieter than usual he sat down at his desk limply, and slowly put on his green eye-shade.

"I have the interview with Dr. Bane, Counselor," Jay said. "You heard about his arrival? He's a crack surgeon, it seems, and he may settle in Culverton or nearby."

"Good. We need a doctor." Phelps nodded. Sweat stood out on his flaccid face. His voice was husky. "Catarrah's bad tonight," he remarked. "I've been taking medicine all day."

He drew out his flask, and tipped it back.

Rogers knew by this time that the 'medicine' Phelps was continually taking was pure, unadulterated whisky. But the boss could hold a surprising amount without showing more than a mellowness. The Counselor also was a well-read man. He loved Shakespeare and often quoted the bard. But the mechanics of writing bored him. It was hard work, so Rogers did most of the labor on the paper.

"You'll give Dr. Bane a front page spread, of course," instructed Phelps. "Play him up. We want him to stay with us, and all that. You know what to say. Let me see what you've written."

Phelps glanced over the copy, and changed a word or two. He handed it back, nodding.

"Very fine, my boy," he said. "You have real talent for this work. We'll keep track of the good doctor and lend him a hand in his own great work."

The Counselor shivered, and drew his coat about him. There were dark circles under his washed-out eyes.

"I don't sleep well," he complained. "'O sleep, gentle sleep, Nature's soft nurse! How have I frighted thee, that thou no more wilt weigh my eyelids down and steep my senses in forgetfulness?'"

"Which play is that from, Counselor?" asked Rogers.

"King Henry the Fourth. You should

study your Shakespeare more carefully, Jay. Nothing like the great bard."

Rogers left before Phelps did. He finished his work, and spent the evening with Della.

He was at the office early next morning. Phelps had not yet come in. The owner of the paper usually slept till noon in his room at the Elite.

Rogers, glancing from the front window as he heard some shouts, saw a cowboy on a brown horse coming slowly along State Street, leading another horse on which a blanket-wrapped bundle was tied. From the shape, from a grisly glimpse of a limp head hanging down, Roberts knew it was a dead man. Electrified, he went flying out the front door, stuffing copy paper in his pocket.

"Found him lyin' in the bush two mile' out on the north road," the cowboy replied to Rogers' questions. "He's am Army officer, I reckon. Got on the uniform."

"Why, it's the major who was at the

hotel yesterday!" Jay Rogers exclaimed.

"Somebody robbed him and stabbed him to death," the cowboy said mournfully.

"I wonder how he happened to be riding out that way," said Rogers. "When I interviewed him he told me he was on his way to Arizona."

The cowboy shrugged, and shifted his tobacco cud.

"'Twixt me'n you, son," he said, "this jasper wasn't killed where I picked him up. Nope, plain as the nose on yore face to a feller who savvies that he was done in and then dumped in the chaparral."

"Outlaws may have held him up and robbed him," said Jay. "I heard a rumor that Frenchie DeLuys had moved over this way from across the Pecos."

The cowboy shrugged noncommittally. "I ain't sayin' who done it, because I don't savvy. I'll run this to the town marshal and let him take over. It's his business."

It was an exciting mystery and Rogers made the most of it for the *Call*."

As the days passed, Dr. Bane received a large share of publicity. Phelps insisted on it, and Bane made good copy anyway. People were coming to him for help, and the doctor built up a practice without trying. He remained at the Elite, but one story Jay Rogers wrote was to the effect that Dr. Bane was seeking to purchase a suitable home.

One morning, two weeks after Bane's arrival in town, Rogers and the settlement were shocked as news spread of another death, that of an old rancher named Horace Youngs who had lived with his wife a few miles west of Culverton.

Youngs' place was in a beautiful setting, with springs bubbling from the hills over the river valley. He had been found shot to death close to his home. Frenchie DeLuys had been seen in the vicinity of Culverton with some of his outlaws, it was learned, and the strain of feared death had fallen over the land.

3

Lone Star Health

CAPTAIN William McDowell stared with a sour face at the large map of west Texas nailed to the wall of his Austin headquarters. Outside it was a lovely day. The windows were open to the scented breezes and a streak of golden sunshine painted the wall with fairy beauty, but McDowell's gloom was not to be dispelled by such picayune allurements.

"Hogwash!" he growled.

The casual observer would have concluded that the good captain, chief of Texas Rangers and responsible for the legal health of the Lone Star State, was in the throes of a horrible attack of dyspepsia. Anyone who knew McDowell, however, was aware that he could not only bite nails but digest them as well.

The only stomach ache he had ever had — physically, that is — had occurred after a rash bandit he had been chasing in his far-off youth had shot him in the midriff. After disposing of the foolish outlaw, McDowell had visited the surgeon, had been sewed up and, it was claimed, had absorbed the ounce of lead by drinking two quarts of frontier whisky.

His intimates firmly believed the tale, except they did not consider that McDowell had really needed any help from the liquor. His natural juices would have done the trick without assistance from the outside.

"Cuss it," he muttered.

He stamped a high-heeled cowboot on the floor so hard that the inkwell fell off the desk, a picture crashed from its moorings to the floor, and the touch-bell rang itself. A terrified clerk gingerly stuck his head around the edge of the hall doorway, not sure whether it was just an earthquake or the captain in another state.

"Yuh ring, Cap'n McDowell?"

"No . . . Yes, cuss it!" roared McDowell. "Ask Ranger Hatfield to report now, right away immejutly."

As he waited for his star officer to appear, McDowell marshalled what facts he had garnered concerning the infected region. Apparently it centered around Culverton, a small settlement in the center of a vast rangeland east of the Pecos.

Forty years before, even a score of summers, McDowell would have leaped on his charger and galloped forth to do battle as physician on the spot. While still good for another decade, as he often comforted himself, age had stiffened much-used joints. The open road, the hardships of the trails, could not be dismissed as lightly as of yore. But his expert knowledge of Texas and her problems of law and order made him extremely valuable at headquarters.

It was not long before a soft tread touched the creaky board just outside McDowell's office. McDowell had ordered that board loosened purposely. He did not like to be surprised in the quarters.

He turned toward the door, and some of the pain left his face. For when Texas was suffering, so was McDowell.

"Hatfield!" he exclaimed. "Yuh made it pronto."

"Yes, suh. I was waitin' for yore call, Cap'n Bill."

"Sit down. I got a sad story."

McDowell took his chair behind the desk, and Jim Hatfield occupied one which was close at hand.

"How's yore health?" demanded McDowell, peering under his hoary eyebrows at the big Ranger.

"Why, plumb fine, Cap'n," replied Hatfield, surprised.

He certainly looked it. Topping six feet, Hatfield had not an ounce of superfluous fat on his powerful frame. He had wide shoulders, his body tapering to the narrow hips of the fighting man, where depended his twin Colt .45s that could spring to action with the speed of legerdemain.

Under his fawn-colored Stetson showed jet-black hair glinting with the health of youth. His gray-green eyes were placid, his bronzed, rugged face composed. Steel, hickory and coiled lightning — that was Jim Hatfield, McDowell's star Ranger, when in a fight.

But in repose his wide mouth was good-natured, and he had an easy way of moving, while his voice was softly drawling. He wore no uniform to mark him as an officer of the State law, but instead wore leather trousers, tucked into black half-boots, a dark-blue shirt, and the usual bandanna to ward off dust when necessary.

To match his physical prowess, Jim Hatfield had a keen mind, trained to the work he did. He had a diplomat's ability to convince men and experience to depend upon.

"I'm fine," he insisted.

"No, yuh ain't," said McDowell, with a wink. "Yore health is bad, Hatfield. What yuh need is a rest in a nice, quiet place like this'n, where yuh can wallow in sulphur water and mud. Take a peek."

McDowell tossed a pamphlet across the desk. Hatfield caught it and read:

Come to Dr. Bane's Culverton Health Center! Here the sick and ailing may bask in the health-giving sunshine and happily return to a new joy of life! Bathe in newly discovered curative sulphur springs. The true Fountain of Youth is here!

Hatfield blinked, as the print became smaller. He knew that McDowell was too shrewd to waste his time, that there was some connection between the booklet and the job to which he would be assigned.

McDowell was ever standing with a skilled hand on the pulse of Texas;

He could detect trouble from afar. For to Ranger headquarters came apparently isolated reports, a robbery here, a shooting there, or perhaps a complaint of sources. When there were enough black spots, mentally tabulated by McDowell in his keen brain, the Rangers must act. Such a point had now been reached. McDowell smelled danger.

Hatfield read on:

Dr. Bane, that famous physician whose practiced skill has been called upon by the crowned heads of Europe, by the famous of New York . . . Now available to sufferers of all classes . . . Native minerals in the earth and waters of the earth, discovered near Culverton by Dr. Bane, assure the sick of a cure if they obey the doctor's orders . . . First-class cuisine . . . Cabins and Rooms . . . Write for Rates or Come to Culverton . . . Nearest railroad stop, Stafford, Tex. Comfortable wagons sent to meet guests on telegraphic orders ... A Frontier Hospital of Distinction.

Hatfield glanced up, meeting McDowell's blue eyes.

"Hogwash," repeated the captain. "However, that's neither here nor there, so long as this Doc Banes behaves hisself and don't rob the folks too heavy. However, I got two kilin's around Culverton. One was a U.S. Army doctor, a Major John Henderson, who was stabbed to death and tossed into the chaparral. The other was Horace Youngs, an old-timer who helped drive the first trail herd out of Texas — I savvied him purty well — was drygulched, seemed by bandits. I got the complaints on these. And then, there's Frenchie DeLuys."

"Frenchie DeLuys?" exclaimed Hatfield. "Yuh mean the outlaw who was operatin' around El Paso? Specialized in robbin' lucky winners at the gambling' tables, I recall. He must have moved."

"Yeah, he's moved — to the Culverton

31

section. He had a close scrape in El Paso when a vigilante committee chased him. I got a half dozen different reports he's been seen in the neighborhood of Culverton. Here's some clippin's from the Culverton *Call*. They say Frenchie may have killed Horace Youngs and the Army medico as well."

And where's this medicine man Bane come in, Cap'n."

"He bought the Youngs' place, with the sulphur springs and magic dirt on it, from Horace's widder. Now yuh savvy I never make up a Ranger's mind for him in advance, but I been settin' here all day, wonderin'. Wonderin' why Culverton gets so active all of a sudden, with kilin's, DeLuys, and a Frontier hospital run by a sawbones good enough to wipe a king's chin for him when he feels bad. That's all."

Hatfield nodded. "I get the point, Cap'n. I'll saddle up and start for Culverton."

McDowell trailed the tall figure to the door.

"Best description I got of DeLuys," he said, "is that he's six feet, wiry as a rat, thick dark hair, frog eyes, and a disposition like a tarantula's. He's left-handed, so watch his left-hand gun. He killed a city marshal in El Paso who didn't savvy."

McDowell watched from the window as Jim Hatfield checked his horse and equipment. He felt pride in his great Ranger, yet he always felt, too, a certain uneasiness when dispatching a man on a dangerous mission. It was his sense of responsibility for the splendid young fellows under his command. And then, he had great affection for Hatfield, who was like his own son. If Hatfield did not come riding back triumphant some day, it would break the old man's heart.

The golden sorrel, caressed by the Ranger's long hand, was a spirited, magnificent animal. Goldy, Hatfield's war horse, had speed and brains to match. Trained by the Ranger, the gelding loved the life of the trail, and carried his friend into and out of perilous situations.

McDowell watched the officer swing easily into saddle. There were iron rations in the bags and a carbine rode in its boot under one long leg, with a belt of ammunition for it attached to the horn. He had his Colts, and plenty of loads for them in the crossed cartridge belts, as well as a knife in an inlaid sheath. The saddle-bags also held clean shirts, moccasins, and other things he might need.

The big hat shaded his eyes from the brilliant sun, and the leather trousers protected his flesh from thorns. On Goldy, Hatfield could travel with great speed through the wilderness. With the gelding as his only comrade, he was able to subsist on the country. He knew the rivers and water-holes, the roads and trails.

With a wave of his hand to McDowell, watching with nostalgic emotion, Hatfield started westward out of Austin.

4

Outlaw Way

HATFIELD was certain that Culverton was not far ahead. On the golden sorrel the Ranger was north of the railraod, off the beaten track, but he was heading straight for that settlement.

The sun was still hot, but it was dropping toward the western hills that were tinged bluish by distance. The air was torpid.

Both horse and rider showed the effects of the long, hard ride they had made from Austin. Gray dust, red dust, other shades of dry, eroded earth had sifted through clothing and accoutrements. It was hot, but Hatfield and Goldy were inured to that. The country through which they were passing was a great plateau, with bare-topped ridges breaking up through its surfaces. These upheavals of rock ran east and west for the most part, with prickly pear growing in the deeper, sandy depressions. Short, curling grasses covered the expanses of red-brown earth, and patches of evergreens, scrub oaks and alders stood out darkly against the general landscape. For twenty miles he had not seen a human habitation.

The road he was on was hardly worthy of the name. It was a rutted track, but the sorrel could move on the grassy lane between the tracks. The trail curved, to avoid a ridge shoulder which turned south before it petered out. This brought the rider past the rise and contours which interfered with his vision to the southwest. He pulled up on the height, and there was a settlement on the snaky, brown river.

"That's her, I reckon," he murmured.

He could see faint smoke patterns from cook chimneys, in the clean, hot sky. Well out from the town, he counted three ranches, several miles apart. Dots meant grazing cattle. Signs of humans — smoke, buildings — were all around.

Pushing on, with the way mostly downgrade for Goldy and easier, he paused again, closer to the settlement. Unshipping his field-glasses he adjusted them to his eyes. He studied the town, and was able to make out the individual buildings, with the setting sun glinting on west windows, and saw the open plaza.

"She looks crowded," he observed.

There were tents set up in the plaza. Westward of Culverton, across the river and in the rust-hued hills, was another plume of smoke.

Dark was at hand when he entered the settlement from the east, through a narrow street which connected with State Street. Oil lamps were being lighted. There were several on posts around the plaza.

Horses and teams were crowded together in the center of Culverton.

Men and women were on the wooden walks, and in the bars and restaurants. Over all was a lively hum, as of busy bees — the interested voices of mankind, the sound of heavy, booted feet, of music in several spots, the neighing and answering calls of horses, the pawing of many hoofs.

A ranch wagon, its axles needing grease, squealed as it drove slowly north on State Street. Cooks banged their pans in the hot kitchens, out of temper with the rush orders. A mingled odor came on the warm wind to the Ranger's nostrils — the smell of sweating bodies, of many various foods cooking, of heated wood and tin buildings, of animals. All the usual odors of a busy town.

Insects, flies and mosquitos buzzed thick in the night. Red lanterns and those of a few other shades mingled with the ordinary colored lights. They gave the settlement a garish aspect. Culverton was teeming with excitement, with men and women who were heedless of everything else except their own affairs.

Hatfield was weary after the trip he had made from Austin. But Goldy needed attention, first of all, so he found a small livery stable on a side street and dismounted, leading his horse into the corral at the side. A Negro wrangler grinned at him, and nodded. The Negro helped the big man groom the sorrel, and after Hatfield had seen to all Goldy's wants, the Ranger thought about himself.

He cleaned up at the pump in the stable yard and put on a fresh shirt. Then he strolled around the corner to find a place to eat. A hot meal would go well after the cold rations he had been living on.

He drifted naturally to the center of things — a hotel and restaurant. The Elite, the sign said, and the proprietor was one Vance Thornton. The lobby was crowded, so were the bar and the restaurant. He managed to push in and get a drink however. Then he extricated himself from the mob and crossed through the lobby to the eating place.

He paused inside the wide doorway, but saw no vacant seat. He turned to nod gravely to the girl behind the cashier's desk. She was a pretty girl, with tight braids of golden hair pinned about her head. Her eyes were large and brown. She smiled at the rugged young fellow.

"You can have a table in a few minutes, sir," she said. "The people in the corner there have nearly finished."

"Thank you, ma'am. Nice town you have."

"Oh, yes. We've been terribly busy lately."

The people were a mixture of West and East. Some who wore range clothing were plainly ranchers and cowboys. Others were clad in the garb of the cities east of the Missouri. Old folks, young, and middle-aged had flocked to Culverton.

It was half an hour before Hatfield

dug his fork and knife into the curled brown slice of fried ham he had ordered. Four fried eggs surrounded it, and slabs of fried potatoes. A large white mug of steaming coffee, with three spoons of sugar, white bread and butter occupied him. The food was delicious, disappeared quickly.

"More coffee, sir?" the waitress smiled at him. She had waited on Hatfield ahead of his turn, impressed by his looks.

"Yes'm. It would top off a fine meal."

Gorged at last, he paid his check to the pretty cashier, exchanged the time of day with her, and went over to the bar. Music came from the annex, and the dance floor was crowded. Doors opening to the rear of the large, rambling Elite showed the way to private gambling rooms.

Hatfield was content, for the moment, to look over the throng when he had finished his dinner. Later he went out for a stroll, to familiarize himself with

Culverton's few streets and ways. He passed a dingy little building on which a sign read; THE CULVERTON CALL. Through the big window he saw a hand-press, and a young man with a green eyeshade hard at work at a desk. As he went by the open door, he caught an odor of ink and paper.

It did not take long to see the sights, which included the marshal's office and the jail, the stores, the several saloons, and the rickety lines of houses.

There were also tents set up on the plaza and in back lots.

He walked slowly back toward the Elite, gravitating naturally to the center of attraction. Finding it cooler outside, he leaned against a dark wall a block away from the hotel, and watched the town.

A man in leather trousers, a brown shirt, and a big gray Stetson emerged from the side door of the Elite. Hatfield idly watched as the cowman ducked under the hitchrack and, picking up his mustang's reins, swung into saddle. He rode north, which brought him past the Ranger.

The rancher was whistling cheerily as he came along.

Three more men, in a bunch, came from the same exit, in time to see the cowman passing a street lamp. Something about their attitude and the guns they wore, drew the watching Ranger's attention. Hastily they picked up horses, and followed the rancher, going on by the corner where Hatfield stood in the shadow.

"Huh!" he thought, staring after them. "They're up to somethin'."

His long legs took him quickly up the sidewalk. The cowman turned toward the road which led north out of Culverton. He was unaware of any danger, but looked around as he heard the *clop-clop* of the horses overtaking him.

"Wait a jiffy, Anson!" called one of the trio.

Anson, the rancher, pulled up. Hatfield

could see his inquiring face as he turned. Then the three were on him. A Colt struck under Anson's nose caught the rays of illumination from the nearest light.

"Fork over that roll, Anson!" the man with the weapon growled.

"Why, cus yuh!" exploded the cowman. "I won it fair and square in the game, boys. Yuh mean yuh're robbin' me?"

Hatfield was hurrying closer, moving along in the shadows of the buildings and awnings which extended over the walk. The harsh voices of the angry victim and the three holdup men came to his keen ears.

"Fork over, or we'll ventilate yore thick skull!"

"All right — all right! Here, take it. But by gee, I'll have somethin' to say to the marshal when I see him!"

"Let the jay have it, George!" snapped one of the bandits.

"No. Don't shoot!" The victim

suddenly realized they meant to kill him, to cover their crime.

A Colt flamed with lurid light. Anson screeched, fell from his saddle to the ground. His mustang lashed out wildly, turned and ran away. But from the Ranger's steady gun a slug had roared, one that had come a breath ahead of George's. The outlaw killer had been hit, even as he raised his thumb off the hammer to shoot Anson.

George slumped in his leather seat. His amazed companions stared at him, for a moment not comprehending what had happened.

The Ranger bored in then, and they spied the tall, dark figure coming at them.

"There he is, Banny, right over there!" howled a bandit. "He plugged George!"

Colts, hastily whipped from leather, were swung on the Ranger. He saw flame as one exploded, felt the wind of a slug passing. But his own pistol had spoken again, and a second outlaw shrieked and lurched off balance. The third and last, horrified at the slaughter of his mates, whirled his horse and galloped off.

Hatfield ran to the spot. Anson, the rancher, was only stunned. Hatfield's quick action had thrown off George's aim, and the cowman was muttering to himself, a hand feeling gingerly at the bloody furrow in his scalp.

Crouched beside the man, Hatfield saw that the robber who had escaped the Ranger gun had turned into a street which ran alongside the Elite. Hatfield jumped up and ran through to the back road from which the saloons and stores were serviced. He was just in time to see the outlaw leap from his horse and burst in through the back door of the Elite.

Ready for anything, Hatfield hurried toward the rear of the big Elite. He ducked back into a recess formed by a store door as men emerged from the Elite.

"Frenchie!" the escaped outlaw was

reporting. "George and Banny are dead! We stopped Anson, and somebody opened up on us from the sidewalk!"

"Frenchie!" thought Hatfield.

He peered down the line, recalling McDowell's description of 'Frenchie' DeLuys, Robbing lucky winners had been DeLuys' specialty in El Paso, so why not here in Culverton? Under the small lamp at the rear door of the Elite, Hatfield saw a tall, wiry figure. He thought that the hair under the curved Stetson was thick and dark. As the leader turned to give orders to the men bunched around him, Hatfield had a glimpse of a vicious triangular face, with black whisker stubble dirtying the sallow skin, and bulbous glowing eyes. Frenchie pulled a colt with his left hand, and McDowell had said that DeLuys was left-handed.

"Who was it?" demanded Frenchie. "What's he look like?"

"Don't know, boss. He was in the shadows on the sidewalk. Looked as big as a barn door to me — and he took only one shot each for George and Banny."

"Circulate," ordered Frenchie. There was a faint suspicion of an accent in his voice, though hardly enough to count. "Hustle and see can yuh find the hombre who done it . . . Hmm, I wonder if big Mike'd dare come in here, after I warned the cuss off."

Evidently the bandit chief thought that a rival might have invaded his present territory.

The gang hurried toward State Street. But the shots had attracted many others, and a crowd had collected about the two bodies and Anson, the rancher, who was still dazed. Frenchie did not join the gathering, although some of his men sifted through the crowd. DeLuys remained in the background, watching.

The town marshal had arrived, and was questioning Anson. Soon they picked the cowman up, and carried him over to the Elite. The outlaws drifted off, picked up horses, and rode out of town.

Hatfield let them go. He was not yet in position to attack, for he needed evidence, connections. He trailed after the curious people who followed Anson into the Elite.

5

New Friends

THE hotel lobby was filled. Anson was laid out on a sofa across from the desk. He wanted a drink and big Vance Thornton, taking charge, ordered whisky brought from the bar. Blood stained Anson's temple but the lamp held in Thornton's hand showed only a swollen, shallow furrow which had scarcely broken the skin of the scalp.

"Better fetch Doc Bane," suggested someone.

Vance Thornton shook his head. "Shucks, it's nothin' but a scratch. Soon as he's rested and had a drink he'll be as good as new."

"That's right, Vance," agreed Anson. "I ain't hurt much. But it was a close call, boys. I thought I'd cashed in my chips."

The Ranger leaned against a doorpost, listening, keeping his mouth shut.

A young fellow with an important air came pushing through the throng, and they made way for him. He was a handsome young fellow, slim, with eager blue eyes. His white shirt was ink-stained, and there was a yellow pencil over one ear. His chestnut hair was crisp, and on his upper lip was the faint smudge of an incipient mustache.

"Another holdup!" he cried. "Say, Anson, did you recognize 'em?"

"Shore, Rogers," Vance Thornton answered, grinning. "You can too. They're lyin' with their toes up in the gutter."

Liquor was brought from the bar, and Anson downed it, smacking his lips. This made some of the bystanders so thirsty they hastily returned to the saloon. Others waited, listening to Anson's story as Jay Rogers drew it out.

"I was in a game with some fellers in the back room, boys," explained the rancher. "I had a big roll, because I sold some cows the other day, and at first I lost, but then the cards come right and I cleaned 'em out. Won four thousand and some odd. I buy a couple of drinks, and say good night, and was hardly started when three fellers who'd been drifin' in and out caught up with me and stuck a gun on me. They took my roll and meant to kill me, for I'd have squealed like a stick pig. Then somebody horned in, opened up from the sidewalk. That's all I remember till yuh picked me up."

"Here's yore cash, Anson. I found it on one of the skunks that was shot."

The speaker was a lean oldster with graying hair and a pepper-and salt handlebar mustache. His blue eyes were sharp and honest, and a five-pointed star marked 'Marshal' was pinned to his brown vest.

"Obliged, Zeke," said Anson. "I'm mighty glad to have it back. I need it.

Rustlers have stole a lot of my beefs lately, and I'm short. Mebbe some of the same bunch as attacked me have run off my cows.

Jay Rogers was taking it all down. "You reckon it might have been Frenchie DeLuys' gang, Anson?" he inquired.

"Might," replied Anson. I couldn't swear to 'em."

"I'm shore one of the dead bandits is George Driscoll," Zeke Tate, the town marshal, spoke up. "Reckernized him from a circular I was sent. It claims he traveled with Frenchie."

"That cinches it!" exclaimed Rogers. "You should arrest DeLuys, Marshal. He comes into town some nights. I'll bet he was here when that hold-up took place. In my opinion, DeLuys and his gang killed Horace Youngs, and perhaps the Army doctor, Major Henderson."

Marshal Tate frowned, riffled by the reporter's implied criticism of his work.

"I got to have evidence to arrest a man," he protested, "and even before that, I got to come up with said hombre, Rogers. You keep shootin' off yore mouth about DeLuys. Some time ago, the *Call* printed a yarn accusin' Frenchie — but I ain't bin able to find a word about DeLuys lately! Talk's cheap. If you kept writin' agin Frenchie, folks might rouse up and deal with him. I'm wonderin' why yuh shut up the way yuh did, in the paper. Couldn't be yuh're scared of DeLuys!"

Rogers gulped and flushed. He had a hot retort on his tongue but swallowed it. There was a laugh among the gathering, and Hatfield was intrigued as the marshal and the newspaperman snapped at one another. Tate winked broadly, grinning as Rogers found no answer to give him.

"The *Call* comes out tomorrer," drawled Tate. "I'll be readin' it all the way from front to back to see what yuh got to say about Frenchie DeLuys!"

54

Rogers shoved his notes in his pocket and thrust his yellow pencil behind his reddened ear. He turned and strode out. The Ranger quietly followed. The reporter interested him. Rogers evidently had ideas about the two killings which had brought Hatfield to Culverton. A newspaperman often had inside information which he might not be able to print but which would be decidedly helpful.

He paused on the sidewalk, in the lurid colored lights from the Elite's bar and dance hall. The music was going, dancers were tripping the light fantastic. Already interest in the hold-up was abating, as men sought their pleasures.

Rogers was hurrying up the wooden walk, toward the *Call* office. His young figure was bent forward and he still looked angry. Hatfield's long legs started to trail Rogers.

He saw the reporter turn into the open door. The office was well-lighted, with hanging lamps about which moths and other insects batted. The Ranger reached the entry, but paused as someone inside cleared his throat huskily.

Seated at a desk was a large, heavy man, with a dish face, sagging jowls and stringy brown hair plastered to his head by sweat. As Rogers stood before him, scowling, the fat man seized a flask and remarked:

"Bad tonight — catarrh's choking me, my boy." He took a long drink, smacking wet lips. "What's the mater, Jay? You look as though your sweetheart had just said nay."

"Look here, Counselor!" the young man burst out. I won't hold back on Frenchie DeLuys any longer. He was in town tonight and some of his men tried to kill Jack Anson of the Double A, after taking his roll. Marshal Tate's sure that one of 'em, killed in the fight, is George Driscoll, a confederate of Frenchie's!"

"I heard the ruckus." The counselor nodded. He thought deeply, then raised the bottle, remarking, "This medicine is good for catarrh. It assists and mildly stimulates the mental processes, my boy." he took a satisfying swig from the flask and smacked his lips.

Hatfield, just outside, could hear the men's voices plainly. Lettered on the window under 'The Culverton Call,' and 'Job Printing a Speciality,' was the legend, 'Counselor Samuel U. Phelps, Prop.' The Ranger concluded that the stout fellow was the editor.

The angry Rogers could not remain silent for long.

"It's an outrage these bandits should be allowed to ride into town and molest decent people," he went on. "This is the third hold-up of the type in two weeks. That cowboy was assaulted and killed on his way home to the Bar Two, after he'd won a few hundred in a poker game. Another man was slugged from behind, and robbed as he lay senseless. They're gettin' bolder, doing the job right in the town. I'll take my oath, too, that Frenchie DeLuys drygulched Horace Youngs!"

"Softly, my boy, softly," cautioned Phelps. "You leap at conclusions, a rash habit of youth. This outlaw DeLuys is a formidable character, a dangerous one. Another killing or two wouldn't weight too heavily on his mind. Do you know what will happen to you — and to me, incidentally, as proprietor of this sheet — if you insist on accusing Frenchie in print and baying the hounds of the law upon him? We'll be immolated, sacrificed *pro bono publico*. You may wish to die for the public weal, but what good would it do us or anyone else for that matter? 'Heat not a furnace for your foe so hot it do singe yourself!'"

Rogers was impatient of the curb. "Never mind Shakespeare, Counselor," he snapped. "Marshal Tate accused us of being yellow, too cowardly to print more about DeLuys. That's how it looks. It's a newspaper's business to help rid the community of such rascals as Frenchie and his bunch."

"True," agreed Phelps. "But you

have only suspicions. You didn't see DeLuys this evening, did you, at the scene of the crime?"

"No. But he sent his gunnies to rob Anson." A crusader's zeal burned in Rogers' young eyes. "I feel like quitting, Counselor."

"Don't do that. Wait till you have sure proof so DeLuys may be held after he's arrested. Come to me when you are certain, and we'll work it out together at the right moment. We don't want to go off half-cocked. That's not good journalism, either. You printed that yarn about Horace Youngs being drygulched by DeLuys, without my checking it first, and you had only hearsay evidence. Some cowboy riding the range saw DeLuys on a horse, the horse left tracks the cowboy believed similar to those left by the killer of Youngs! That sort of thing won't stand up in a court."

"It does with me," said Rogers sulkily. "I have a hunch DeLuys has connections in Culverton, else why should he keep coming here?"

Phelps drew in his breath, as he stared at Rogers. The older man was skillful at argument and he had a hold over his assistant. There was an undercurrent of harshness in his thick voice as he answered the reporter.

"Jay, you've done a good job here. Doc Bane says he's especially pleased with the booklet advertising his Frontier hospital, and he's a good customer for us. Others have spoken highly of you, as well. I depend upon you. However, I'm still the editor of the paper."

"That's another thing," said Rogers quickly. "I wrote that stuff, believing Dr. Bane would be a great benefaction to the town and community. But he's actin' very high and mighty, they say, and his prices are awfully steep. Now, I wonder."

The counselor shook his head disapprovingly.

"Come, come. You need a good sleep, Rogers. Here's what to do: We'll run the story about Anson tomorrow, of course, and quote Marshal Tate on the subject. I'll take care of it. You run along, and you'll feel better in the morning. Then we'll talk it all out."

He reached for Rogers' notes. Jay Rogers stood still for a moment. Then he shrugged, "Good night, Counselor," he muttered, and started for the open door.

As the reporter emerged, Hatfield was strolling up the walk, but turned to follow Rogers who went toward the Elite. Rogers had a swift gait, almost a trot. He was always in a hurry, and Hatfield's long legs had to run before he overtook the young man.

"Jay Rogers!" he said. "I been lookin' for you."

Rogers turned on him, staring up into the tall Ranger's rugged face, touched by the light from a street lamp.

"What is it, sir? Aren't you a stranger in town?"

"That's right. My handle's Jim Hart. I'm from Dallas way."

Hatfield thought it best, for the time, to hide his true identity even from Rogers, of whose good faith he was convinced by what he had observed and overheard.

"What can I do for you?" Rogers was on guard as he kept watching the tall fellow.

"They told me at the Elite — that purty cashier girl did — that you're all right, and on the paper. I wanted to palaver with yuh about this Frenchie DeLuys. Any place we can talk, quiet-like?"

Rogers jumped. He wasn't sure yet of Hatfield, but the mention of the bandit caught him.

"Come over to my room," he said. "We can talk there."

Rogers boarded up the way, across the plaza from the Elite. He had a nice room opening onto a yard by a private door, so that he could come and go at late hours without disturbing the family. He lighted a candle lamp on the table, and turned to his visitor.

There was a single cot in the room which his landlady had made up neatly. There was a table with an oil lamp and the candlestick, a commode, a rag rug, a rocking-chair and board shelves to hold books. Stacks of papers stood in the corner — Rogers' reportorial works. On the walls were the framed pictures, of an elderly couple, his parents, and a smiling portrait of a young lady whom the Ranger recognized as the cashier at the Elite.

"Have a drink, and a cigar," said Rogers, pulling out the rocking-chair for his caller. The chair creaked under the Ranger's weight. "Now," asked the reporter eagerly, "what about Frenchie?"

"This has got to be confidential, for the time bein'," stipulated Hatfield. "No printin' it in the papers."

"All right." Rogers was still wary, but a newsman gathered his tips from such contacts, and he did not wish to miss out.

"Well, first I pulled in here just after

dark, Rogers. I come to Culverton on purpose, because — well, Horace Youngs was my uncle. When I heard he'd been drygulched, I decided I'd run over and revenge him!"

Rogers drew in his breath. Vendetta were familiar to Texas and the rest of the South, and this yarn lurid enough to catch his writer's fancy.

"I see. You came to the right spot. Your uncle's killer is near here."

"That's what I figger. I heard yore set-to with that town marshal. But I ain't connected in these parts — yet. I thought I'd have a word with you first of all, since yuh seem all right. I'm trustin' yuh. I didn't want to go to the law, yuh see, direct-like. The marshal's prob'ly got funny ideas about takin' care of Frenchie legal-like."

"He has. I'm certain DeLuys caught your uncle near his home and shot him in cold blood, for the few dollars he had on him. It was like this: Danny Freylinger, who rides for Jack Anson's Double A, was in the posse which tried to trail Horace Youngs' killer. They lost the tracks in the monte but they saw enough so that Freylinger could remember the horse's sign. Freylinger told me that a short time ago he spotted Frenchie DeLuys on a big black gelding, a fine animal. He picked up the tracks later and they matched those leading from Young's body! Add to it that DeLuys, who has a large gang at his command, has been waylaying winners from the gambling tables, and in my opinion it's cinched."

"Mine, too, Rogers. I think I seen DeLuys tonight!"

"You did! Where was he?" Rogers was eager.

Hatfield cleared his throat, glanced around, and lowerd his voice.

"It was like this. I was standin' in the shadders up from the Elite, when I see a rider come along. Three caught up with him, and they robbed him and started to down him. Before I realized it, I'd opened up and two were kickin' on the ground! The third rode off, and

I run too. I hustled around back, just in time to see the bandit feller meet a tall, frog-eyed hombre with black hair, who drew a Colt with his left paw. Mebbe that's Frenchie?"

"It certainly was!" Rogers could scarcely contain himself. His eyes shone, and he danced up and down. "Hart, you're a hero! The whole town's lookin' for you, because you saved Jack Anson's life. This is too good to keep!"

"But yuh'll have to hold it while, Rogers. We don't want to warn of DeLuys. I kept my mouth shut because I didn't feel like answerin' a lot of questions from the law and others, savvy? But you put me on the right trail and I aim to skin DeLuys and nail his hide to the fence!"

"I'll help you," Rogers declared eagerly. "I believe DeLuys has friends in town, which is why he keeps comin' back. I'll bet that in a day or two, when the Anson business quiets down, Frenchie will sneak in again after dark and try another robbery."

Hatfield nodded. "That's where me'n you come in. We'll trail him till we catch him red-handed. Right?"

"Right! I'm with you."

Rogers hated to let Hatfield go. A look had convinced him of the Ranger's fighting prowess, to say nothing of the story concerning the scrap that evening. He made Hatfield whom he knew as Hart promise to hunt him up the first thing in the morning.

Then they parted, the Ranger going to sleep in the livery stable where he was keeping Goldy.

6

A Trap for Frenchie

NEXT morning was beautiful, sunny and warm. A west wind brought the scent of sage and evergreens. Jay Rogers and Hatfield sat at the same table at the Elite for breakfast, and Della Thornton waited on them herself, it being early and the place not yet crowded with customers.

It was plain to Hatfield that the girl and Rogers were deeply in love. The glances they exchanged, the way they spoke to one another, even though the words meant nothing in themselves, told him this.

"Yes, business has been boomin' here." Rogers nodded replying to the Ranger's probing. "It's on account of Doc Bane. He's a famous physician who's opened a Frontier hospital near town. People have flocked to Culverton on that account. Bane has some wonderful warm sulphur springs, and the minerals in the earth around here help sick folks get well."

"I saw a circular last evenin', Jay," observed the Range. "Yuh believe that hogwash?"

Rogers squirmed and looked rather ashamed. "Well, I did when I wrote it. Bane told me it was so, and my boss — he's Sam Phelps, owner of the *Call* — agreed. Anyway it's been a great thing for the town."

"How about the folks who spend their money up at Bane's?"

Rogers gulped down some coffee. "Well — I've thought of it some. Bane isn't as decent as I believed at first. His prices are awfully high. He did set a leg for one of Jack Anson's riders who got crushed under a horse last week, but sent Anson a big bill."

"Where is Doc Bane's?"

Rogers blinked. "Why, it's right over there west of town, in the foot-hills.

Don't you know where your uncle's home was?"

"You mean Bane bought the old ranch?"

"That's right — from your aunt."

"Well, strangle me and throw me in the crik! Yuh see, right after we got the wire sayin' Unc was dead, I lit out, and I missed hearin' Auntie had sold out."

"Oh!" The exclamation satisfied Rogers.

The reporter had to go to work, at the *Call*. He made the Ranger promise twice that he would meet him in front of the Elite that evening. He feared that the tall man might slip away and fail to return, and thus wreck a great story.

Hatfield saddled up the rested golden gelding, and rode off across the wooden bridge spanning the river. The road led up through rust-hued hills, and after a few miles he saw a fresh-painted sign on a wagon trail to his left, which read:

He moved in, but did not go directly to the place. Instead, he took a side path and climbed a height. Breaking through a patch of pines, he saw the hospital stretched below him. It was a former ranchhouse, but work had been done to enlarge it, and new barbed wire fence surrounded the building and the acres near them.

The house was roomy, hugging the ground as it nestled in the hills. There were many tents and cabins lined along the brown-watered pools, the sulphur pools from which a warm mist rose in the morning air. Patches of trees and brush, and some gardens, broke the rolling surface. Smoke came from the chimneys, and from smaller fires.

He adjusted his field-glasses, and studied Bane's place. He could see men and women, some in dressing gowns, reclining in chairs, or lying in the sun. Others were bathing in the warm spring. The house, formerly

71

Horace Youngs' home, had a long veranda running around three sides. One wing, from its new look recently attached to the large *hacienda*, had iron bars in the small windows, bars cemented into the adobe wall.

For an hour, the Ranger lolled on the hillside, observing. In that time he saw people he could tell were patients. He concluded that others, men in white pants and shirts, were attendants. Some Mexican men and women could be seen through the open kitchen doorway or when they emerged for a brief spell to empty garbage — cooks, he decided. There was a stable and corrals, where riding horses were kept, a corncrib, storehouses and other shacks, besides the tents and cabins. Around all was the gleaming, three-strand barbed wire.

Hatfield was in no hurry. He did not wish to show himself around Culverton too much during the day, until he had made his plans. He unsaddled Goldy and took it easy in the shade, now and again focusing his glasses on Bane's.

It was near noon when he saw Counselor Samuel Phelps, editor and owner of the Culverton *Call*, ride up to the gate in a buggy. He was immediately admitted to the hospital grounds, and stopped at the front, getting down and dropping the anchor, an iron weight attached to a strap which would keep the horse from moving off.

A small man in a blue suit and wearing a straw hat came over and shook hands with Phelps, who put an arm familiarly across the little man's shoulders as they went up the steps and inside.

"Wonder if that's Doc Bane?" mused Hatfield. He yawned. The heat was gratifying, and his lids drooped.

He checked the trails in sight, the lay of the land, before he saddled the gelding and rode back toward Culverton. Upriver he undressed and had a bath in the brown waters. It was dark when he entered the settlement.

He met Jay Rogers as they had

agreed. They wasted the next four hours, until midnight, on a fruitless watch for Frenchie DeLuys, but the outlaw chief did not appear in Culverton. It was twenty-four hours later, close to the stroke of twelve, before Jay Rogers found his new friend, the tall man in the dark area near the Elite.

"Jim!" he exclaimed in a low voice. "Frenchie DeLuys just went into Pedro's. I'm sure it's him."

"*Bueno*. C'mon, and show me."

Pedro's was a Mexican's *cantina* at the south end of State Street, two blocks from the Elite. There was a large front room, with a dirt floor onto which oil from smoky lamps had dripped, and the odor of kerosene mingled with that of *tequila* and cheap whiskies. Benches and slab tables, a long plank set on two barrels, made up the bar.

"They're in back," whispered the excited Rogers.

Circling, they came up stealthily to the rear of Pedro's. Half a dozen horses, reins to the ground, stood with heads down at the dim-lit open doorway. Men were sitting in the private room at the back, and a Mexican with a dark moustache who was wearing a white apron and muddy boots, was serving them with drink.

From Hatfield's vantage point across the narrow byway, he could see them through a raised window. One was the black-haired, frog-eyed Frenchie DeLuys, the man he had glimpsed two nights ago.

"Let's keep close watch, Jay," he said softly. "Mebbe they'll try their old tricks agin."

It was a tiresome wait, however. DeLuys and his toughs, heavily armed bravos — two of them Mexicans, the others of Anglo-Saxon, German or Irish strains — were thirsty. It was a warm night and they had been riding hard. Glass after glass of *tequila* went down the hatch. Their voices, which had been low and considered before, grew raucous and louder. They talked chiefly of women, and their conquests, boasting.

At one-thirty, a man hurried in to whisper in Frenchie's ear.

"Hey, fellers!" sang out DeLuys, discretion gone with sobriety, "some cow nurse just won three thousand at Vern's roulette wheel! C'mon and I'll show yuh how to handle it. Driscoll bungled the job the other night, but watch yores truly."

As the drunken outlaws emerged, Hatfield and Rogers remained hidden. They saw DeLuys start unsteadily along the narrow back street, trailed by several cronies, two of whom led the horses.

"Hadn't we better call the marshal for help, Jim?" whispered Rogers, as Hatfield, keeping the stables and other outbuildings between them and the enemy, flitted after DeLuys.

"Follow me, Jay. We can take care of it."

Up the way, the bandits paused. One of them held the mustangs, while DeLuys and the others cut between two darkened stores to State Street. Hatfield, with Rogers at is heels, hastily circled. They took another passage to the main street, and were but four buildings up from the shadowed recess where DeLuys lurked.

Vern's was a gambling parlor north of the big Elite, on State Street. Music and the rollicking voices, the general howl of the crowded Frontier settlement, filled the night. A knot of cowboys emerged from Vern's singing, 'For he's a jolly good fellow!' They were slapping a drunken friend on the back — the cowboy who had made the lucky strike at the roulette wheels. He was a lean young man and he was grinning from ear to ear, happy over his good fortune.

"So long, boys, so long — got to find my hoss!" he cried.

His acquaintances returned to the bar, after the parting, and the cowboy lurched up the sidewalk, ducked under the hitch-rack, and moved along the gutter, talking to himself. Earlier in the evening he had parked his mustang in front of another saloon and was trying to recall just which place it had been.

Late as it was, there were men and women on the streets, Culverton was enjoying an unprecedented boom.

Few noticed the cowboy, however, beyond a passing glance.

DeLuys was watching from his niche when the cowboy located his horse not far from the point where the outlaws were concealed. Hatfield and Rogers, peering, saw the tall DeLuys hurry out, duck under the rail, and move on his prey. One man went with the bandit chief, and three grouped on the sidewalk to watch and keep guard.

"Take this Colt, Jay," ordered the Ranger. "When I hit, you fire on the three standin' on the walk, savvy?"

"All right, Jim."

Hatfield crossed the walk in a shadow line. The standing mustangs hid him as he hurried up, his Colt up and ready for action. DeLuys had caught his victim just as the cowboy was picking up his reins and the bulk of the horses hid them from chance passers by.

"Reach and fork over the cash, cowboy!" ordered DeLuys. He had drawn up his bandanna, and he was backed by an armed comrade.

"Why, you sidewinder!" gulped the cowboy, but his hands flew up over his Stetson.

"Pull his fangs and take his roll," ordered DeLuys.

It was Hatfield's moment and the tall Ranger lashed in. He meant to arrest DeLuys, so he struck the outlaw an expert blow with his Colt barrel. DeLuys fell at his feet, and the other bandit whirled with a curse.

The sudden attack had surprised them. Hatfield fired a breath ahead of DeLuys' companion, who staggered back, gasping for air, before he went down under the stamping hoofs of a startled mustang a few feet away.

The trio on the sidewalk whipped their guns. They had seen the charging, dark figure of Hatfield, silently boring in. The Ranger threw himself around and knocked the cowboy, who was a bit slow reacting, off his feet, out of the way. He fell in the dust, as slugs from the guns of the three outlaws shrieked overhead.

But they could not fire downward without hitting DeLuys, over whom the Ranger crouched, his gun swinging. Flaring, heavy explosions began from the dark recess as Jay Rogers, obeying instructions, emptied his cylinder in the direction of the group on the walk.

"Run for it — it's a trap!" shrieked a befuddled gunny, and he and the others tore away, taking the first turn off State.

Shouts rose down the way as the booming guns rang through Culverton. The Ranger turned the senseless DeLuys over with one hand as Jay Rogers came hurrying to his side.

"You got him?"

"Here he is, Jay. Pronto, fasten his hands before he wakes up." Hatfield's voice was low, urgent.

The cowboy, whom they had saved from being robbed of his winnings, and probably from a beating or even death, was sitting up, rubbing the dirt from his eyes, and swearing a blue streak.

"I'm duckin', Jay," continued Hatfield. "You stick here and turn DeLuys over to the law. See yuh later."

"But — "

"Do me a favor and don't argue now. I'll be around."

Men were running toward the scene, and the Ranger ducked under the rail to the walk, and slid away. He observed from a distance as townsmen, including Marshal Zeke Tate, arrived on the spot. He could hear the babble of voices, and Rogers' excited explanation.

Any rescue of Frenchie DeLuys was now impossible, for a crowd had collected. The cowboy, sobered by the close squeak he had had, was vociferous in accusing the prisoner, whose hands Rogers had fastened behind him, using DeLuy's own kerchief, torn from his face.

The outlaw who had sided him was dead, killed by a Ranger bullet. Zeke Tate picked up DeLuys, assisted by willing hands, and they carried the unconscious Frenchie over to the lock-up. Hatfield, trailing along to make sure there was no mistake, watched as Tate opened the little cell block and threw Frenchie into one of the three small cubicles.

"Now," mused the Ranger, "we'll soon find out who're DeLuys' friends in Culverton."

7

A Bandit's Friends

IN the morning Jim Hatfield was breakfasting with the delighted Jay Roberts, when Counselor Samuel Phelps came into the dining room and approached their table. They had already made sure that the chagrined Frenchie DeLuys, his head aching and a dark-brown taste in his mouth, was still safely lodged in the jail. Marshal Tate had slept in his office all night, guarding the prisoner.

"Good morning, Jay, my boy," boomed the counselor.

"Morning, Boss. You're up early."

"'This morning, like the spirit of a youth that means to be of note, begins betimes,'" quoted the counselor. He made a wry face. "I had a poor night, Jay, a poor night."

83

"Sit down and have some coffee and cakes. This is a friend of mine, Jim Hart."

Phelps nodded, glancing at Hatfield, but he was more intent on his thoughts.

"I will not stay now," he said. "I just wanted to ask you to come to the office as soon as you're through your breakfast. I hear that last night you captured an outlaw — uh, the very bandit, DeLuys, we were discussing the other day."

"Yes, Counselor. We've got him cold this time. He can't escape. I saw the hold-up with my own eyes, and Ed Spear, a KL cowboy whom DeLuys tried to rob, can testify as well. DeLuys can't wriggle out of the charges. He'll get ten to fifteen years for robbery. I'll be right over, and get the story ready for our next edition."

"Very good. I'll be waiting for you."

Phelps nodded. The bags under his eyes were dark, and he coughed hoarsely as he waved a pudgy hand and walked slowly out.

"He's mighty interested in DeLuys, ain't he?" said Hatfield.

"Yes. I've wanted to flay DeLuys and his gang in the paper but the boss has been leery. Such fellows sometimes come after an editor who's attacked 'em, and gun him without warning. But now the sheriff can hold DeLuys and convict him. I'd better get on over to the office. I'll see you later, Jim."

The Ranger let him go. Dell Thornton smiled at Rogers, and he paused for a minute to chat with her on his way out. When he had gone hastily off down the street, Hatfield followed. The morning sun was losing its redness as he stood on the sidewalk and saw Rogers enter the newspaper office. Then Hatfield strolled down, quietly, and leaned near the open door. Rogers and Phelps were arguing.

"But Chief, we've got DeLuys pinned to the wall!" cried Rogers.

"He's dangerous, I tell you. We'll be slaughtered. Do as I tell you, Jay. Soft pedal the story. Say he was drunk and in a playful mood, that it was disorderly conduct and he should be let off with a fine. After all, he didn't get away with the cowboy's money. Who laid DeLuys out anyway? Did you?"

"Well — I helped." Hatfield had exacted a promise from Rogers that he would not expose the supposed Jim Hart. "Ed Spear and I both saw the hold-up with our own eyes."

"As a favor to me, Jay, forget what you saw, and let's not act like fools."

"What about Spear?"

"He'll be taken care of. Anyway, what Spear does won't hurt us." Phelps spoke with a tense earnestness. "You'll see. DeLuys has friends who won't let him be sent to prison. They'll go after Spear and us too if we don't keep our mouths shut."

Rogers' voice was filled with disgusted anger. "I'm not afraid, and I'll tell the truth. You may kill the story for the paper, but I'll go on the stand against DeLuys. That's final. I'm ready to quit the job if you insist."

"No, don't be so hasty, Jay. I — I'll think it over." Liquor gurgled in a flash, as the counselor sought a stimulant.

Hatfield saw Vance Thornton, the big Texan who was owner of the Elite, emerge from the salon and come toward him. He moved slowly to meet Thornton.

"Howdy," Thornton said, and smiled as they passed each other, and the Ranger murmured a polite greeting.

Thornton turned into the *Call* office and Hatfield sauntered back. He could always say he was looking for Jay Rogers if anybody cared to ask.

Thornton had a voice as strong as a bull's. He could be heard a block away.

"Dell told me yuh'd been in and wanted to see me, Counselor," he said. "I was out back. What can I do for yuh?"

"Sit ye down, Thornton," said Phelps. "Have a snifter to dispel the morning vapors." he called, "Oh, Jay! Will you please run over and ask Marshal Tate if he has any fresh news items for us?"

Hatfield stood his ground. Rogers came out, and the Ranger touched a finger to his lips, took the reporter's arm and they stood together, listening as Phelps talked with Thornton. Though surprised, Rogers had learned to do as his new friend wished.

"I have a favor to ask of you, Vance," began the counselor. "The *Call* has done you some services in the past. We've always spoken highly of you and the Elite. 'Splendid hostelry, serving only the best to the best!'"

"That's right, Phelps," boomed Thornton. "We all owe a lot to the *Call*, for helpin' the town grow. E'rybody's makin' money, what with Doc Bane's shebang and all. It's been a fine thing, all the advertisin'. I'll do anything possible for yuh."

"It's about this bandit, Frenchie DeLuys," said Phelps. "You have a great deal of influence here, Vance. Last night, as you no doubt know, Frenchie was arrested by Marshal Tate and lodged in jail. I wanted to ask if you'd try to have the charge changed from robbery to disorderly conduct. You can do it, I'm sure."

"What!" Thornton was amazed. "But Phelps! This DeLuys is a notorious robber and outlaw! If they strung him up it'd be only what he's got comin'. I'm surprised at yuh."

"I'll tell you frankly, Vance, I'm afraid. Afraid of being shot in the back by DeLuys' friends. This boy who works for me — Rogers — is heedless and thoughtless, like most youths, and he's put the *Call* in a bad spot by attacking DeLuys, Now he's actually helped capture him and means to testify against him." Phelps cleared his throat. "I understand that your pretty daughter, Della, is much interested in Jay. They make a fine couple, don't they? It would hurt her terribly if anything happened to him. You see, I'm thinking not only of myself but of Jay."

"Huh! I — I didn't figger it

thataway." Vance Thornton was brought up short as he saw the possibilities.

Hatfield had hold of Rogers' arm. He could feel his young friend trembling, trembling with angry excitement.

"I'll think it over, Counselor," promised Thornton. A chair scraped. He was about to leave. "'Course, on second thoughts, a man's got to be a man and face things." Thornton's voice was drawling. "I don't mean you, Phelps, but Jay Rogers is young and tough."

"Not tough enough to stop a killer's slug, Vance."

"Yeah. But somebody has to rid the country of skunks like DeLuys. I ain't exactly loco to horn in to protect a no-good bandit."

A chair scraped again and Thornton emerged. There was a queer look on the Texan's red face as he saw Rogers standing there.

"Howdy, Jay — howdy agin."

"Look here, Vance!" cried Rogers. "I heard what Phelps said and I want you to know I didn't ask him to protect me! I'm not afraid of Frenchie or anyone else. If you fix it for DeLuys — well, then you're no friend of mine."

Thornton's eyes lighted and he began to grin. He slapped the angry Rogers on the back.

"That's the talk, Jay. Glad to hear yore spunk. As for me, I got no intention of speakin' a piece for DeLuys and his kind." Thornton strode back toward the Elite.

"C'mon, Jay," suggested Hatfield, "let's go have a drink."

He dragged Rogers off, and shortly they stood together at the Elite bar.

"This boss of yores, the counselor," said the Ranger softly, "ain't got any nerve to speak of, Jay, or else he's got some good reason for puttin' in a word for Frenchie DeLuys. Can yuh figger it any other way?"

Rogers squirmed uncomfortably. "I — I don't know, Jim. I hate to talk about a friend behind his back."

"And that's only right and proper.

Still, sometimes a feller makes a mistake in a friend. It's happened to me."

"Phelps is old and he's not very well, Jim. It isn't so terrible for him to be afraid of what the outlaws may do to him."

"True. But he can keep anything he don't want to print out of the paper. In that case, why does he ask Thornton to fix things? That's goin' out of his way to be careful."

"I — I'll have to think," muttered Rogers. "I'm goin' over to my room for a while. I'll see you later."

The Ranger hung around through the warming day, observing the town. Frenchie DeLuys languished in the little jail and Marshal Zeke Tate was constantly on hand, guarding the building. Many people had come to Culverton to enjoy the famous hot baths as advertised by Dr. Jonathan Bane. Some lived in the settlement and drove out to the Frontier hospital for treatments. There were still others who had come to serve and make money out of the crowds.

Interested in the reactions of Counselor Samuel Phelps to the arrest of Frenchie DeLuys, Hatfield kept out of sight and quiet as far as possible.

In the afternoon, after the worst heat of the sun had declined, Jay Rogers drove a hired buggy up to the Elite, and went in. He came out with Della Thornton on his arm and helped her into the buggy. They rode off together into the country. Rogers was upset and Hatfield decided the young reporter had gone out to talk over the situation with the girl he loved.

It was nearly six o'clock when Hatfield, in the Elite bar, saw Marshal Tate bang through the batwings. The officer was excited, and his strong voice boomed resoundingly through the saloon:

"Boys! I just had word from a rider that the KL is bein' attacked by a passel of masked bandits! I need a posse — forty, fifty men — pronto. Who'll volunteer?"

Tate had friends, young fellow in town he could count on in an emergency, and as he pointed at one after another, the posse was rapidly made up.

"KL," mused Hatfield, as the marshal rushed back toward the office. "Why, that's the outfit Ed Spear works for!"

Spear was a vital witness against Frenchie DeLuys. Excited by the news, the big Ranger quickly hustled out and rapidly saddled Goldy.

He moved toward the jail and marshal's office, where Zeke Tate was swearing in his deputies en masse, while a helper passed out ammunition.

"Hur-ree, hur-ree, Marshal!" fumed a dark-hided Mexican who had brought the alarm.

He worked for the KL spread, which lay about twenty miles northeast of Culverton. He had been out to pick up some horses and from a hilltop had seen the attack begin, so had ridden for town at once.

94

"Need an extra gun, Marshal?" asked Hatfield.

"No, I got enough . . . Well, c'mon, then." Tate had sworn in fifty-five men, but as he looked up into the gray-green eyes he decided one more would help. He did not know Hatfield, though he had seen him round town the past day or two. "What's yore handle, young feller?"

The Ranger replied:

"Jim Hart. I'm a pard of Jay Rogers."

"*Bueno*. I see yuh got a good hoss. Pinky'll give yuh ammunition." To the posse he said, in a stentorian voice: "All right, boys! Mount and let's ride. You lead the way, Pedro, till we get there."

'They're after Ed Spear, so's he can't testify agin Frenchie,' thought Hatfield, as he left Culverton among Tate's posse, bound for the KL.

8

Realization

JAY ROGERS felt cheerier, more sure of himself, as he drove back to Culverton with Della Thornton at his side. They had gone down the river road, south of town, and had stopped on the bank of the stream to talk. The hours had flown and it was sundown when Rogers pulled up the team in front of the Elite and jumped down to help the girl out.

"Do as I say, Jay," advised Dell. "You must be honest with yourself."

"I will, Dell," he promised. "It was a help to talk to you. I'll see you later."

She smiled and hurried in, for she was late. She had taken the afternoon off, as had Rogers, to enjoy the buggy ride.

Rogers ran the team around to the livery stable where he had hired it. The talk with Della had done a great deal of good, he mused. Her womanly intuition had seen through artificial barriers his mind had built up. She had said that no matter what he felt toward Counselor Phelps, that if his employer did wrong, then Jay must part with him. While she did not wish Jay to take unnecessary chances — that was understood — he could not be a coward.

"I'll have it out with the boss tonight," thought Rogers who was deeply under Della Thornton's influence.

There was another influence which had lately come into his life — that of the big man he knew as Jim Hart. Rogers had been tremendously impressed by the man's fighting prowess and looked upon the Ranger as a first-class ally.

Hatfield had planted the seeds of suspicion against Phelps in the reporter's mind, and they had sprouted quickly.

Originally, Rogers had ascribed the counselor's unwillingness to attack DeLuys in print to physical fear of the consequences, but Hart had hinted that Phelps might have other motives.

Thinking it over, Jay realized that he knew little of Phelps' former life, before the counselor had hired him for the *Call*. Phelps had turned aside natural inquiries which Rogers had made. Everything he had ever said had been general, such things as that he had had legal experience and newspaper jobs in other parts of the country.

Phelps had lived quietly, drinking a good deal when Jay had first come to work for him. When Dr. Bane had come to Culverton the counselor apparently had not previously known the physician, but they had rapidly become friends.

The livery stable man greeted Rogers jovially.

"Howdy, Jay. Enjoy the run?" He winked, knowing how Della and Rogers felt about each other. "Say, you missed

98

a lot of excitement. A passel of masked evils attacked the KL late this afternoon, and Marshal Zeke's done rode out with fifty or so possemen to give 'em a chase."

Rogers jumped. "The KL! That's where Ed Spear works!" He, too, immediately jumped to the conclusion that the attackers were friends of Frenchie's trying to destroy the witness against DeLuys.

Gleaning what details he could from the stable proprietor, Rogers hurried over to the *Call* office, but it was dark.

"I'll find Phelps and see what he has to say about this outrage," he decided. Then he recalled the counselor's word concerning an attack on Spear. "He was mighty sure of it."

So far, Phelps had proved right. It was a dangerous thing to be a witness against DeLuys.

Rogers galloped down the street to the Elite. Phelps was not in his room or in any of the public places. The reporter kept an eye peeled for his tall friend, Jim Hart, but did not see Hart either. Della, at the cashier's desk in the restaurant, said she had not seen either Phelps or the big fellow.

Puzzled, Rogers went outside and stood on the sidewalk, undetermined as to what he should do.

"Maybe I ought to ride out to the KL and see what's going on," he was thinking when he looked up the street and saw an elegant equipage that was stopped in front of the *Call* office.

From it came Counselor Phelps' stout figure, and that of a smaller man. Rogers recognized his employer by the street lamp's light, and thought the other man was Dr. Bane. They went into the newspaper building and as Rogers started toward the *Call*, a light came up inside.

The front door had been closed. Rogers knocked sharply. A burly figure moved from behind the big carriage — it was Bane's rig — and came quickly up.

"What yuh want here, mister?" demanded the driver.

"I'm Jay Rogers. I work here."

The door opened and Phelps looked out. He saw Rogers standing on the stoop, with Bane's man just back of him.

"Oh, good evenin', Jay. What is it? I'm busy."

"I wanted to talk with you," replied Rogers. "There's a boldfaced attack being made on the KL, where Ed Spear lives."

"Yes, yes, I heard of it. Plenty of time for the news, though. We don't publish till Thursday, you know." Phelps was rather short with him, but went on in a more kindly tone. "You go home and get a good night's sleep. Or go see Della at the Elite. We'll talk it over tomorrow."

"But — "

"Tomorrow, I said." Phelps started to close the door.

Rogers could look past the bulk editor into the lighted office, and in a comfortable armchair where Phelps often liked to relax, sat Dr. Bane. The little physician wore expensive clothing — a black frock coat, gray trousers, and a pearl-gray velvet vest. A glittering stickpin was thrust into his silk stock, and he leaned on his silver-knobbed walking-stick.

The door slammed and Rogers, disgruntled, stared at its blankness.

"Move along, feller," the driver of Bane's carriage growled. "You heard what Phelps told yuh."

Rogers was burning with anger. As he turned impatiently he saw another man, a footman, leaning against the carriage wheel.

"Take your hand off my arm," he snapped. "I'm going."

He walked off down the street and went into the Elite. At the crowded bar he had a drink, but he was much perturbed, and quickly went out the back way. Ordinarily he would have thought nothing of Phelps wishing to talk privately with a friend, but Hatfield had aroused his suspicions.

"I'm going to find out what all the secrecy's about," he muttered.

The rear windows of the *Call* office were open. He tiptoed close in, and leaned in the dark shadow of the wall. Dr. Bane was sitting there in the office, talking with the counselor. Bane took a silver snuff-box from his coat pocket, and extracted a dainty pinch between his thumb and forefinger. He sneezed violently several times. Phelps paused in his talk until Bane had finished his snuff.

Then the counselor resumed:

"I hope you're right, Bane. But you know my line isn't violence."

"You don't need to tell me that, Sam," snapped Bane. "On other jobs together I soon found *that* out!"

"I can't help it, friend," Phelps said miserably.

"I know, I know." Bane's voice last its rasp. "You've done a good job here, bringing in the suckers. The paper was a brilliant idea of yours. We've never been so well-set."

Rogers' heart seemed to flutter in his breast. He was astounded to hear Phelps and Bane speaking familiarly.

'Why, they're old friends!' he thought, his fists clenched. 'What sort of jobs do they mean?'

It dazed him and his head swam.

"Violence is sometimes the only way out of a bad situation," Bane was saying. "It saved us from that fool major. You tried to free DeLuys, through Thornton and your other influences, but it didn't work, did it? Now we must try the only other recourse — and at once. Everything is arranged."

Phelps cleared his throat. A bottled gurgled, as he sought to fortify his quailing soul.

"You think they got Spear this afternoon?"

"I'm sure of it. How have you fared with young Rogers? I hope he has sense enough to do what you wish."

"Well — perhaps I can prevail on

him. I have a weakness for the lad, Bane. He's a hot-headed young fool, but you know how association with someone makes you feel."

We can't afford to take chances, Sam."

"True. But I wish we hadn't had to hook up with DeLuys. The jackass, getting caught that way, right in the act! They're usually reckless, such fellows."

"But we had to have the connection. DeLuys supplies us with vital protection here, and he comes in extremely handy when someone like Youngs gets in our way. We owe him reciprocal aid."

"Not only that, but he'll squeal like a stuck pig if we don't save his hide," growled Phelps. "Why try to sugarcoat the pill?"

Jay Rogers, his horrified soul stunned, picked up each crumb let drop by the two inside.

"Why, they're up to a crooked game! Suckers, that's what Bane calls the people who come to him for help.

He's making a fortune, and he's a thief and a faker, too! No real doctor would talk this way . . . I — I helped bring patients here, too. I'm guilty of helping Bane!"

Weak and sick from realization, Rogers could not yet figure out the entire pattern. He passed a hand over his face. He was physically ill.

Intent on the talk inside, he was too late as he caught a faint tread close at hand. A powerful hand seized him by the back of the neck, as he swung to fight back.

"What you doin' here, snoopin'? Oh, so it's you!" The burly driver of Dr. Bane's carriage had caught Rogers eavesdropping. "Didn't Phelps tell you to get?"

"Let go of me!"

Rogers hit the man in the nose. The hand loosened its grip on his neck and he tried to duck under and away but a foot neatly tripped him, as Dr. Bane jumped up and came to the window.

The driver fell on Rogers, a knee

driving into the small of the reporter's back, and his cries were choked off.

"What's going on out there, Lon?" demanded Bane.

"It's that young Rogers hombre, Boss," puffed Lon, who was having a time holding Rogers down. "Burke thought he seen somebody back here so I sneaked around and cause him."

There was a brief silence, then Bane ordered coldly:

"Fetch him in. Just shove him through the window, Lon."

The little doctor had a pearl-handled revolver, with a short silvered barrel, in one hand, and his stick in the other. Lon lifted Rogers bodily and thrust him inside the newspaper office.

"Jay!" cried Phelps, also on his feet. "Have you gone mad? Why were you listening out there?"

Quiet, Sam," commanded Bane. "I'll handle this."

Rogers, his back wrenched from the kneeing, his breath gasping from the tussle and from excitement, faced them, a wild look in his eyes. He had seen Dr. Bane a number of times, but he hardly recognized the usually benign face. The black eyes snapped, and Bane's upper lip and hawk nose twitched. A red glow burned in his gaze, while myriad little lines had deepened in his brow. The features and muscles stood sharply etched in the yellow light that came from the lamp.

"I — wanted to talk to the counselor," Rogers said lamely.

"You suspected us. That's why you sneaked back to listen to what was said. My men have orders to keep a sharp watch for snoopers. You've made a serious error, Rogers. You're playing with dynamite. However, Phelps is very fond of you. I'll give you a chance to prove yourself, but you must come in with us."

"All right," said Rogers quickly, thinking he might worm his way out and call the law.

Bane was staring at him, his eyes burning into the reporter's.

"You may prove yourself tonight, and now," he said. "Marshal Tate left a guard, old Baldy, at the jail when he rode out this afternoon. I'll give you a gun and you will shoot Baldy dead. This will show me you mean what you say."

Rogers thought quickly, but there was no way out. He squared his shoulders. 'Don't be a coward!' Dell had said.

"I meant to quit the job, Phelps," said the reporter. "I was pretty sure you had a good reason for helping Frenchie DeLuys. Now it's obvious. Bane and you are a couple of rascals and dangerous ones. You used me as a tool, to write for you and bring unfortunate people here so you could cheat them out of their money at the hospital . . . You're a faker, Bane. I wonder if you've ever been a doctor, really."

Bane shrugged. "I have no time for the small egotisms of an unimportant person such as you, Rogers. Because Phelps likes you I offered you a chance, which you've flouted.

Heavy gunfire suddenly smote the night air. It rang over the plaza, echoing back from the faces of the buildings. Confused shouts, and a shrill screaming began, and the drum of mustang hoofs shook the earth.

Bane's black eyes widened.

"Here they come, after Frenchie!" he cried. "I want to see it!"

He sprang forward, straight at Jay Rogers, and without further warning slashed the reporter with his heavy cane. Rogers went down. Lights sprang to his eyes, he felt the violent smash of the metal knob, and then all went black.

9

The Coward

AS Jim Hatfield galloped toward the settlement, under a rising moon, he heard the gunfire in Culverton.

"I Reckon my nose didn't fool me when I smelt a rat!" he muttered, and begged Goldy for more speed.

He could guess what was happening, and regretted the natural impulse he had obeyed when he had been stampeded out of town by the alarm. For with Marshal Zeke Tate and his formidable posse, he had reached the KL after dark. It was a comparatively small ranch, hiring a dozen riders, one of whom had been Ed Spear, witness against Frenchie DeLuys.

When the citizen force had arrived, all was over. They were informed by the owner, Keith Lee, that without warning Ed Spear had been drygulched, then about twenty masked rustlers had opened fire on the surprised ranch. Lee and his men had fought them off. They had just ridden away, no doubt aware of the posse's approach.

Tate had done the natural thing, again — what any competent law officer might do. He had picked up the fresh trail, which led roughly westward, and stuck to it. For a time, Hatfield had been swept up by the excitement of it and had tagged along, but as the country had grown rougher, the going more difficult, the outlaws had split up into several smaller bands. Cooling off, Hatfield felt less and less urge to keep on.

Doubts began to grow more insistent in his analytical mind. Why had the attackers, after disposing of Ed Spear, the witness against Frenchie Deluys, made no determined effort to rush the place, even after dark? If they had not wanted to fire the stables or the house, in revenge and perhaps to rob the owner, why hadn't they ridden off after killing Spear, instead of lying in cover and besieging the ranch?

They must have seen the Mexican wrangler on the run that afternoon, and known help would be rushed from Culverton. They had been watching for a posse's approach. Yet they had waited till the last minute, and then left a clear trail, running just ahead of Tate.

The posse had paused to check the sign and to give the horses a breathing-spell, and to let stragglers catch up. Hatfield had approached Marshal Tate.

"This looks like a draw-off to me, Marshal," he said. "If yuh want my advice, I'd say we ought to head back to town."

But Tate had shaken his grizzled head. Others wanted to keep going, and so the Ranger had turned and hurried back to Culverton alone.

He flew on now, the wind whistling past his ears, his Stetson brim flapping. The shafts of moonlight touched the rugged, set fighting jaw. Black shadows of trees, and of serrated rock spires on is right, rapidly broke the silver shine, while the dips let it through again. He was aware of the kaleidoscope effect as his eyes registered the changes of light.

Culverton, with its vari-colored lamps, spread before him, as he galloped into the settlement. On the plaza were many riders, and dismounted figures as well, close to the jail. The jail was dark, but from a front window flame of a shotgun showed that somebody in there was fighting.

As Hatfield, his colt drawn, rushed on, he noted among the hoarse shouts and shriller voices of frightened women across the way, a dull thudding. At the rear of the lock-up was grouped a knot of men who drew back, in unison, and then drove forward together, again and again. They had a heavy log with which they were smashing through the cell-block adobe wall. Old 'Baldy,' who had been left in charge in Tate's absence, coud not cover all sides, and bullets smashed thick through the window at which he as crouched.

"There she goes!"

Hatfield saw them throw down the battering ram, saw the black hole made in the cell wall. Several of the masked outlaws reached over the pile of rubble and helped a man outside, hurrying him to the waiting mustangs.

There was a brief gunfight at the breach. Old Baldy, brave as a lion, tried to keep them from rescuing the prisoner, Frenchie DeLuys, but they were too many for him. His shotgun went off, but after the answering blast from the enemy, Baldy's weapon did not again object.

Now the big Ranger was almost up. He raised his Colt to fire into the massing gunnies. There were outriders, watching for just such interference. He saw the orange-red flames of spurting guns turned his way, as they tore around to cover him. They were starting off with DeLuys in the other direction, riding south from Culverton. A few citizens, among them Vance Thornton, had armed themselves and were shooting from behind rain barrels and the bulk of buildings, but the outlaws were on their way.

It would be sure death, with no objective to achieve, if Hatfield rode straight into the blaring guns of the ready enemy. He swerved, aware that lead was too close for comfort. A slug ventilated his Stetson crown, and others kicked up dirt near the sorrel's beating hoofs. The rear guard which flashed across the plaza, shouting, firing at the elusive figure, cut him off, and turned him. A hasty citizen fighter, going off half-cocked, tried for the Ranger, thinking him one of the bandits.

Dust and acrid powder smoke drifted in the warm night air over the plaza. The outlaws had gone south, but turned at the crossroads and the hoofs of their horses drummed on the loose planks of the river bridge. The rear guard, lying back to cover the escape, moved slowly after the other. Hatfield, cutting through a lane and circling the buildings, could not beat them to the bridge.

"No use," he muttered.

His grim face was stained with dirt and powder grime. His Colt was burning in his hand. He had made hits, he knew. A dead bandit lay in the plaza and others had carried off Ranger lead. But others had snatched DeLuys.

Goldy was lathered, for the golden sorrel had made the run to the KL, partaken of the chase, and then returned to Culverton. In such a case even the greatest of animals must have rest. Besides it would be easy for DeLuys' men to lie in wait at a turn, and blast him if he tried to pursue in the darkness without careful checking at every curve.

He swung Goldy, and the sorrel walked wearily back into the settlement.

Vance Thornton and others were at the jail. A silence hung over the gathering. They had carried out old Baldy, who had died in the breach, trying to prevent them from taking his prisoner. Old Baldy lay there, riddled. They had got him when he had showed in the opening, furiously fighting to the end.

"Pore old Baldy," growled Thornton. "He was a good hombre."

Baldy had on old black pants, a dirty black shirt, and his boots were run down at the heel. His face, set in death, was bewhiskered, but his dome was as bare of hair as a marble, shining in the lantern they had brought. Around his ears, white fringes stuck out like shelves.

Vance Thornton recognized the tall man who came up.

"Howdy, Hart . . . Say, didn't you ride with Marshal Tate and the boys?"

"That's right. I come in ahead of the main bunch, though. Them outlaws killed Ed Spear and shot up the KL, but run when we showed up." Hatfield's voice was slow, quiet.

"Must have worked a trick to draw Tate and our best fighters out of town," said Thornton. "Well, fellers, we might as well pick up pore Baldy and get him ready for burial. There's some carrion on the plaza, too, needs to be put underground so it won't smell up the town." Thornton's face was brick-red. He was angry because of the flagrant attack, and because of Baldy's death. "By hook, fellers, we've got to clean them polecats out so's we can call our souls our own," he snarled.

There were lights on in the Culverton *Call* office. Hatfield strolled that way, after a drink at the Elite. A carriage stood at the curb, and a couple of men, evidently the drivers, lounged nearby. The door was open, and he went on by as he saw that Dr. Bane was in the newspaper office, talking with Counselor Phelps. He circled the town afoot, for Goldy was in the stable resting, after having been rubbed down.

Jay Rogers' room at his boarding house was dark, and the door was closed.

'He must be out, seeing this excitement,' he mused. He could not recall having seen the reporter in the crowd at the jail, however.

But Rogers had a habit of tearing from one spot to another and the Ranger didn't take alarm when he did not immediately find the reporter. He eased back to the Elite for another drink. The restaurant closed for the night, and Della Thornton was behind the lobby desk,

She smiled at the tall man, whom she knew to be Rogers' friend.

"Jay?" she repeated, in answer to Hatfield's query.

"Oh, yes, he was around not long ago. He took me for a drive this afternoon and we didn't get back till supper time."

"Reckon I'll bump into him soon. Thank you, ma'am."

The Ranger was tired after his long

ride. He had another drink, a smoke, and then he went to the stable and turned in, sleeping until the following dawn.

What roused him was the return of Marshal Tate. Tate had been going all night and his eyes were red and his face covered with sweated dust. Some of his men came with him, and bunches straggled in for the next hour.

"Hey, you, Jim Hart!" Tate hailed the Ranger, as the tall man slouched across the plaza in the cool morning air. "By glory, yuh was right about that KL business bein' a draw-off — and to get Spear as well. Wish we'd took yore advice and come in last night!"

"You wouldn't have made it in time, Marshal, I reckon," replied Hatfield. "Lot of yore posse's mustangs was played out."

He was still looking around for Jay Rogers. He went on, and knocked at the private door to the reporter's room. There was no reply, and he tried the knob, stepped inside. The bed was made up, and the young man was not there.

The *Call* office was not yet open for the day. Phelps was asleep in his room at the Elite Hotel.

Hatfield went into the dining room and ordered his favorite food — ham and eggs, with coffee and rolls on the side. The young waitress who attended him liked the big man and chatted with him, standing at his side while he ate and marveling at his capacity.

Others began drumming on the tables for service. The place soon was filled with Tate's deputies whose appetites were wolfish after the long chase.

Hatfield paid his check to Della. Her face was pale, her long lashes covered her eyes, and she could not smile up at him as usual. She held her body stiffly.

"Jay been in yet?" he inquired.

She glanced up quickly then, and he could see that she had been weeping. She looked away and shook her head. A brash cowboy, behind Hatfield, pushed a hand in and laid a ten-dollar bill on the counter with his check.

"How about change?" the waddy smiled at her.

The Ranger went outside, rolled a quirly and smoked it in the warming sunlight. Then he walked to the *Call* again, but the padlock on the door was still unopened.

'Huh, that Jay Rogers has sort of hid hisself,' he mused.

He was beginning to feel uneasy over Rogers. Della's attitude puzzled him. Why should she have been crying? If anything had happened to Rogers, she would have told him, instead of behaving as she had.

'They didn't get him last night, that's a cinch. I'd have heard if he'd been kidnaped or shot down by that passel of devils.'

Vance Thornton was in his barroom when Hatfield entered it. The hotel man looked glum, and he was short with the inquiring Ranger.

"Rogers? Ask Della." He shrugged.

His face was beet-red. "I ain't interested in the cuss."

Hatfield went back to the dining room. In a lull at the cashier's desk, he tackled Della again.

"Ma'am, I got to find out what's happened to Jay Rogers. Now don't shake yore purty head at me. It's important, I know. Did he get hurt in the mess last night?"

No, that wasn't it. Hatfield has been pretty sure it wasn't, but he hoped to start her talking. She was still pale and she was still mourning, no longer outwardly, but weeping in her heart, he was certain. At last, under the spell of his soothing, soft voice, and the Ranger magnetism, Della reached in her apron pocket and brought out a small note. It had been crumpled up, but she had smoothed it out. Spots showed that she had dropped tears on it.

"You can read it, Jim," she said in a small voice. She was ashamed, her woman's pride crushed with her soul.

It was a hasty scrawl on a sheet of *Call* stationery and read:

Del,

After what happened tonight I'm beaten. They'll kill me next. Won't tell you where I'm going but maybe I'll be in touch with you sometime.

                                                    Jay

Hatfield was deeply shocked.

"He — he left it on the desk, in an envelope with my name on it," Della told the Ranger faintly. "Then he ran away. I — I don't blame him so much for being afraid. Anybody would have been. But the way he's done it is too much."

"Yes'm. I got to think this over. Thanks."

Hatfield went out, crossed to the bar, and joined Vance Thornton.

"She told me, Vance, showed me the letter," said Hatfield.

"Yeller, that's what," growled Thornton. "I didn't believe he was. He run because he was shore the DeLuys gang'd gun him. He was the only remainin' witness agin Frenchie on that Spear job. I told Della it's just as well she discovered it before they got hitched. But nothin' comforts her. Have another drink."

Thornton was tanking up, to drown his sorrows. It was sheer torture for the father to see Della so unhappy.

"Cuss his hide," Thornton snarled. "I'd like to wring his scrawny neck! The whole town savvies they had an understandin', and they'll say he jilted her!"

"Perhaps it won't be that bad," Hatfield said, for he knew that a slight error could be built into a wild story by more talk about it. "Some people might think that Jay did the wise thing. It's not fair to call a man a coward until he's proved one."

10

Impatient Patient

BEFORE the fat, sloppy figure of Counselor Samuel Phelps appeared in the lobby, ten o'clock had rolled around. Hatfield was lounging near the desk.

"Phelps," Thornton said, "yuh savvy that reporter whelp of yores took French leave?"

Phelps' jowls waggled as he nodded. His face lugubrious.

"The poor lad," he said sadly. "I can't find it in my heart to blame him. I've felt like running myself. The outlaws may come after me next. Last night Jay came to me terribly upset because of the attack on the jail. It was the last straw for his overwrought mind. He told me he couldn't stand the gaff longer and was leaving before

127

they killed him. Everything seems to be going wrong lately." The counselor sighed. "As the good bard puts it, Vance, 'When sorrows come, they come not single spies, but in battalions . . . One woe doth tread upon another's heels, so fast they follow!'"

Shaking his head, Phelps waddled to the dining room to get his breakfast.

Hatfield went over and leaned on the desk. "Wonder what time Rogers pulled out, Thornton? Yuh see him go?"

"Nope. If I had, I'd have hogtied the sidewinder and beat his nose in."

"He dropped the letter to Della on the desk. Yuh here then? Did he have anything to say?"

"Huh? No, I wasn't here. I found the note, addressed to Dell, lyin' on the blotter when I come in late."

It was only a straw, but the Ranger wanted to grasp at such. He prided himself on being a good judge of character, and Rogers running away in such cowardly fashion simply did not jibe with his settled opinion of the reporter. Jay had proved courageous in a pinch, when they had gone after and arrested DeLuys.

He went back to the restaurant. Counselor Phelps was eating an ample meal, and reading from a leather-bound volume as he enjoyed his repast.

'Shakespear, I s'pose,' thought the Ranger.

He had had suspicions of Phelps, ever since the editor had intervened with such determination in behalf of Frenchie DeLuys. Now he meant to keep a close eye on the man.

Hatfield leaned on the cashier's desk, and smiled at Della.

"I'm checkin' up, Dell," he said, his voice low. "Did yuh see Jay when he dropped that note on the desk? Anybody tell yuh he left it hisself?"

"No. I was in charge while father was out. Jay must have watched for a chance to come in when I was in back or upstairs, and left the letter then."

"It's his handwritin' — yuh savvy it?"

"I haven't seen too much of his writing, Jim. It wasn't necessary for him to write me letters, though he did send me a couple of poems." She flushed as she admitted this.

"Did Jay own a hoss?" he inquired.

Della shook her head. "He always hired a rig or a mount at Terry's, down the street. I suppose he got one there last night."

"Do me a favor. Let me borrer Jay's farewell note for a while. I'll fetch it back."

"All right. But I don't see what good it will do."

The detective strain in Hatfield was at work, hunting the faintest clue. A Ranger had to be possessed of such powers, as well as physical prowess. He pocketed the little note and went down the street to Terry's livery stable. He spoke briefly with the proprietor, a friend of Rogers.

"Nope, he didn't git a hoss from me," said Terry. "He might have picked one up somewheres else, though."

Back at the Elite, Thornton could not say where Jay Rogers had obtained the mount on which to flee Culverton. None had been reported taken from the street rails, and Thornton did not know of anyone having lent a mustang to the panic-stricken reporter.

Over at Rogers' boarding house his landlady was equally at sea. Rogers had not slept in his bed and his things were undisturbed. Under the Ranger's persuasive sway, she took the big man into the reporter's quarters.

Rogers' two carpet-bags were unpacked, and in the closet. His things lay around — his pipe, clothing, even a small sum of money on the commode. On the table was a small book marked, 'Diary for the Day.' The landlady, a motherly woman who was much worried about Rogers' fate, looked over Hatfield's shoulder as the Ranger opened the record.

"I want a look at the writin', ma'am," he excused himself, as he perused Rogers' diary.

131

"Oh, yes, he writes such cute things," the landlady said, smiling. "Specially about Della Thornton."

Hatfield blinked, and grinned to himself. Evidently the landlady's womanly curiosity had been greater than her ethical sense, for she had been reading the reporter's personal book. His own eye stopped at a passage which read:

This day I met Jim Hart, a really marvelous fellow. What a fighter! I'd go to Hades and back, with him at my side. Single-handed he saved Jack Anson's life and bankroll! So he told me and I believe him. He seems a bit mysterious, too good a fellow to have just wandered here for revenge because of his uncle, Horace Youngs.

Hatfield had the note lent him by Della, and he compared the hand-writings.

"Sort of roughly alike," he mused. "'Course, a man may write funny when

132

he's upset, but there's real differences . . . Now, I wonder!"

The landlady, her neck craned until it seemed a foot long, was trying to read the note over his hunched shoulder.

"You're Jim Hart, aren't you?" She beamed when Hatfield caught her at it. "Jay spoke of you as his new friend. He was so fond of you, and he wrote so lovingly about you, too! Is it so that you're a nephew of Horace Youngs? He was an old friend of mine." She simpered and blushed, "In fact, I could have been Mrs. Youngs, I do believe, if I'd had a mind to!"

"Yes'm, I don't doubt it," agreed the Ranger, secretly amused. "You're a beautiful lady." He patted her hand, and she smiled up into the gray-green eyes.

When he left Rogers' quarters, the mystery had only deepened. He would have liked to question Counselor Phelps, who was now over at the *Call* office, hard at work.

'But I don't wanta alarm him,' he thought, 'Looks like he scares easy.'

Outside of Phelps, Hatfield could find not a single soul in Culverton who had seen Rogers leave the settlement or heard him say he was going. He sought some subterfuge by which he might approach the editor, and finally decided on one.

The counselor was at his desk, a quill pen in hand, and with a green eye-shade on his forehead as he wrote copy. In back, an oldish man, the printer who assisted in getting out the paper each week, was setting up type in a form.

Phelps turned and nodded in a friendly manner to Hatfield. He had seen the tall fellow around town with Jay Rogers. His washed-out blue eyes with the little red flecks in the whites, fixed themselves on Jim Hatfield.

"Well, young man, what can I do for you this bright and lovely morn? Have you a sprightly news items, a tit-bit of gossip, for my paper? Or do ye desire to advertise your wares?"

"Nothin' like that, suh. I got a grievance. Folks claims that Jay Rogers has run out of town, and I come here because this is where he worked. He borrered twenty-five dollahs from me at the roulette wheel the other night and I want it back."

Hatfield's tone was injured. His expression was sour and he drooped.

"Sorry, my boy, very sorry. I fear your money has flown on the wings of ill-chance. Rogers departed without leaving a forwarding address." The counselor's husky voice dropped as he cleared his throat. "Confound catarrh," he complained. "It chokes me up. Excuse me. I must take my hourly dose of medicine."

He drank from a flask, and shoved a decanter toward the Ranger.

"Here, have a drink, and forget your bad fortune. Money lent is money lost. Let it be a lesson."

Hatfield made a wry face, put a hand to his stomach.

"I feel turrible, and yuh'll have to excuse me. I need the money, though I still got some. Seems like a bunch of leetle devils are doin' a fandango in my stomach. I come here because I heard it was good for the health, but I don't feel no better'n I did. A mule kicked me last year and I ain't been the same since."

"I see. You should consult Dr. Johnathan Bane. Just coming to Culverton won't cure all the ills of a man, you know. You no doubt need to partake of the healing mud baths, and be properly physicked."

"I've heard of Doc Bane. I was thinkin' I'd go see him. Yuh reckon he'd charge much to talk to me?"

"That depends. As the good bard puts it, 'Diseases desperate grown by desperate appliances are relieved, or not at all!' You're acquainted with W. Shakespeare, young man?"

"Oh, yessir," nodded Hatfield. "Met up with him in the Red River country."

"Eh?" Phelps was startled, and he

blinked as he glanced quickly at the Ranger. "You say you've met Will Shakespeare?"

"Shore. I was punchin' cows for the Triple Y, and this hombre mooches along and stops overnight at the bunkhouse. He had a wagonful of books with him and told us he was sellin' 'em to earn money so's he could get an education and support his widered mother. He admitted he'd wrote the book — it was marked by William Shakespeare, too. So the boys all bought a copy, includin' me. I kept it a long while, till one winter we run short of paper on the ranch and the boss's wife tore out all the pages to use. I ain't much on readin', of course, or writin' either, for that matter."

The counselor was secretly amused by the character the Ranger had assumed, that of an ignorant, hypochondriacal cowboy. Phelps maintained a grave demeanor, however, as he shoved a volume of Shakespear toward the visitor.

"Is this the book you purchased?" he asked.

Hatfield handled it clumsily, upside down.

"I ain't got my glasses with me, suh, he said, passed back the book, and went on, "I do take a lot of stock in writin' though. It'd be mighty pleased if yuh'd give me a few lines tellin' the sawbones who I am."

Phelps hesitated. "Dr. Bane's a very busy person. Have you as much as ten dollars left?"

"Oh, shore. I got a couple hundred. I saved my pay a long time. Yuh see, I been feelin' bad and aint gone out on sprees."

"Them by all means go consult Bane," Phelps said quickly. "No finer healer exists. Here, I'll give you a piece of writing, as you suggested."

On a sheet of *Call* paper the counsel scribbled hastily:

To Dr. Bane: Sir, this will introduce —

He paused, to say, "Your name has slipped my poor memory, my boy," and as Hatfield gave him his alias, wrote on:

James Hart, the bearer, sad possessor of a troubled digestion. For my sake, do not make the charges Two High.
                                         Phelps

He passed it gravely to Hatfield, who made a pretense of being unable to read it.

"Thanks a million!" cried the Ranger. "I just can't wait to be cured."

"An impatient patient," punned the counselor. "I wish you luck in your quest for precious health."

"Yes, suh. And thanks agin."

Slightly doubled over and with a dyspeptic's troubled expression on his rugged face, Hatfield limped out. A short time later he rode out of Culverton on the sorrel, headed for Dr. Bane's.

As he rode in the warm Texas

sunshine across the river bridge, with the boards drumming hollowly under the shod hoofs, he talked in a low voice to the golden sorrel.

"I'm shore, Goldy, that Phelps wrote the note s'posed to have been left by Jay Rogers. Phelps dropped it on the hotel desk when nobody was lookin'. The writin' in the letter he give me to Doc Bane has important likenesses. 'Course, he done his best to imitate Roger's hand . . . Phelps is mighty tickled with his own jokes. He spelt 'too' wrong, made it 'Two', and a big 'H' after it means *two hundred*, what I said my roll was! Took me for a big fool, like I hoped he would . . . Him'n Bane're in cahoots, no doubt of that."

He had some blank paper. He creased it and, with his sharp hunting-knife, carefully cut it to the size of greenbacks. He wrapped his real paper money about the dummy and had a sizable roll.

11

The Face in the Window

WHEN Hatfield reached his destination, the gate stood open. A couple of men were lounging in an open shed as the Ranger came up. A large sign on two sturdy posts read:

DR. BANE'S FRONTIER HOSPITAL
DR. JNO. BANE, PROP.

The men were big fellows who wore white pants and shirts. Their keen eyes scrutinized the rider. There was a bulge under the left arm of each man, probably made by hidden six-shooters, thought Hatfield.

"What yuh want, feller?" demanded the stouter guard. He had black hair, dark eyes, and a hard mouth. His lips went sideward when he spoke, and he wasted no politeness on a cowhand.

"I come to see the doc," replied Hatfield.

"Huh? You're a cow nurse, ain't yuh? Work for one of the local outfits?"

"No, I come a long ways, because I heard tell the doc's a wonder and might cure me."

"Now look here. Doc Bane's a busy man. He can't be bothered with ev'ry itch and sore toe somebody might have. Why don't yuh ride on over to Stafford and see the sawbones there?"

"Well, I sort of counted on Bane," replied Hatfield mildly. His way was as soft as his voice, and his attitude hide his true power. "Fact is, Counselor Phelps give me a letter to the doctor." He took the note from his shirt pocket and handed it to the big guard.

"Why didn't yuh say so before? Yuh can come in."

The gateman whistled shrilly, and a Mexican youth came riding from the buildings behind the main structure.

"Take this hombre to the office, and see that Doc Bane gets this letter," ordered the guard.

"Thanks a-mighty, boys," said Hatfield gratefully.

He trailed the Mexican youth, and stopped outside the front of the big house. It was as he had observed it through his glasses from the hill, during his first visit. The ranchhouse had been enlarged; the adobe bricks had been freshly whitewashed and the walls gleamed in the sunlight. There were people down by the sulphur springs and mudbaths, and the tents and cabins were set some distance from the house.

He could scent the odors of the place — the food cooking in the large kitchens, and other familiar smells. Barbed-wire fences hemmed in the main ranch. Here and there, an unobtrusive man, in the white pants and shirt such as the gatemen wore, could be seen.

To the left of the main front door

was a private entry. Over it was a gold-leaf sign:

OFFICE. PRIVATE. DR. BANE

Behind the office was the attached oblong wing which had steel-barred windows.

'Got a real set-up here — plenty of money in it,' thought the Ranger, as the Mexican guide disappeared inside with the note.

Soon the youth emerged. He smiled, and motioned Hatfield to go in to the private offices. Hatfield dropped his reins, and stalked up the steps. The door was open and he went into a large, cool room with heavy blue drapes hanging at the windows. The light was dim, and easier on the eyes than the blinding sunlight. A young woman smiled at him from a desk.

"Dr. Bane will see you soon, sir. You're Mr. Hart, aren't you?"

"Yes'm."

It was a twenty-minute wait before

a bell rang, and the young woman jumped up and went to the inner sanctum door.

"You may go in now, Mr. Hart," she said.

Hatfield limped slowly through the door, and stood on a thick carpet before a long desk behind which sat Jonathan Bane. The smell of a doctor's office — drugs, mingled chemicals — clutched at his nostrils, and from the corner of his eye he saw a high, black leathered horsehair couch, some forceps and saws, and bottles of colored solutions. In the corner his startled glance encountered a skeleton suspended by a golden wire.

But it was the small man behind the desk who seized and held the Ranger's attention. Dr. Bane was watching him, his wiry body relaxed in his large chair. He wore a frock coat despite the heat, and a white stock at his throat. Myriad little lines radiated from the corners of his intensely black eyes, he had a hawk nose, a strong personality,

145

and shrewd analytical power which Counselor Phelps entirely lacked.

The Ranger knew he must make no slips, take no chances with Dr. Bane.

"Good afternoon, sir," said Bane. He had a cool, quick way of speaking as he sized up the patient. "Your name is Jim Hart, according to Counselor Phelps' letter. I'm a very busy man, and wouldn't have been able to see you, ordinarily, but I am doing so at Phelps' request. Now, just what is your trouble? Please make it as brief as possible."

"Yes, suh, I will. I got kicked in the middle by a mule three years ago last fall roundup, yuh see. I had a misery there ever since. I read about you and figgered I better come see yuh. I feel powerful bad sometimes, Doc." Hatfield's voice was mournful, his pose perfect.

"Yes, yes . . . Just lie down on the couch. Loosen your belt and shirt . . . That's it."

Bane moved with a flea's agile speed.

Before Hatfield knew it, he was flat on his back on the horsehair sofa and Bane was probing with strong, long fingers at his innards.

"Hurt there — no? Here? No? Here?"

"Ow, ow-w!" howled the Ranger, doubling up. "Doc, it kills me!"

Bane frowned, stepped back. "H'm, just as I thought. Young man, you have a serious internal injury, a plague of the spleen and upper ventrical umbilical."

"Yes, suh, Doc," gasped Hatfield. "Is — is she fatal?"

"It may prove so, unless you receive immediate and proper treatment. You'll need massage — I have a skilled assistant here who can give that — and soothing mud baths. A diet besides, and medicine I will prescribe. In this way we may be able to heal the tear which is giving you such pain. Also I may apply leeches. I cannot got too far in warning you of the gravity of your condition."

"I — I reckon it's terrible, Doc. I don't want to die. I'm too young. How

147

much'll all of it come to?"

"Let's see. You must remain here at least two weeks. I'll have a small tent set up for you near the baths. With the medicines and my fee, I'll make it two hundred dollars. Phelps asks me to help you or it would be much more."

"That's mighty white of yuh, Doc." Hatfield buttoned his shirt and hitched up his trousers. He reached in his pocket and peeled money off his apparently large roll. "This is for the first whirl. I'll pay the balance tomorrer."

"Very well." Bane returned to his desk. "My secretary will have your medicine ready this evening. Good day, sir."

'Doggone,' thought the Ranger, as he found himself outside and shy twenty dollars, 'if I didn't feel so all-fired good, I'd believe I was sick! He's mighty convincin'.'

There was a corral where he turned out Goldy. He wandered slowly through the fenced grounds of the hospital, maintaining his invalid's air and pose. Unobtrusive guards were about, and other patients, with the self-engrossed look of the chronic invalid, were completely absorbed with their symptoms and troubles.

Many had come from far off, nosed by Bane's high-pressure publicity campaign. On the Frontier there was little if any control over such fakers as Bane. The sun was dropping behind the western slopes when an attendant in a white outfit found Hatfield, and showed him to a small tent with a cot in it. This would be his home while he was there. He would take his meals in a large, open-air shed, furnished with board tables, with the bulk of the patients.

'He's shore got organization,' mused Hatfield, as he dozed in the sun after looking over the grounds. "And there's a fortune in it for Bane. He's cleanin' up."

There was power, Bane's power, everywhere in evidence. The Ranger saw the man strolling near the office, with a thin oldish man, white of hair, and with a peaked face.

"Wonder who that is?" he thought.

The older man had the appearance of one who had been hearty, an outdoor person, but had wasted away in sickness. Bane had an arm about his shoulder, and talked with him animatedly.

"Bane thinks a lot of him, evidently," decided the Ranger.

Soon a bell rang, and the rank and file shuffled to the tables. The food was wholesome and palatable enough, and Hatfield tried to eat twenty dollars' worth. He did not see Dr. Bane or the patient with the white hair and peaked face at the common tables, and concluded that the proprietor, and perhaps special guests — those with extra money — probably ate in Bane's private quarters.

The last light of day found the Ranger stuffed to repletion, smoking a quirly behind a tree. He did not wish to appear too healthy in plain sight. A carriage came up the circling driveway, and Counselor Phelps slowly emerged, puffing from the exertion. Hatfield put out his cigarette, and sang out to the editor who turned to wait for him.

"I got here, suh," said Hatfield, hurrying up. "And I'm mighty grateful to yuh for that letter. It done a world of good. Doc Bane says I'm in an awful fix but he figgers he may be able to save me for a few years."

"Well, well — glad to have been of service. A beautiful spot here, is it not? Reminds me of a little piece your personal friend Will Shakespeare tossed off, no doubt to buy a meal for his widowed mother: 'I know a bank where the wild thyme blows, where oxlips and the nodding violet grows . . .'"

"He was a smart hombre. Wrote purty things, didn't he? I do wish I could've read some."

"One thing at a time," said the counselor. "First you must get well, my boy."

"Oh, Phelps!" Dr. Bane, who had emerged from the office door, sang out sharply to the editor. "Will you please come in at once? I have some important business."

"Yes, Doctor, at once . . . All right, James, I will see you anon. Keep away from mules." Phelps smiled and waddled up the steps to go inside with Bane.

"Now what?" thought the Ranger. "I'd like to get inside them private quarters, and hear what goes on."

Slowly he moved away. He could not appear to be nosy, or arouse suspicion. There were watchful guards about, and one was turned his way even now, as Hatfield glanced back at the barred windows, three of them in a line.

He was startled as he saw a white face appear for an instant, pressed against the steel bars. He was aware of tortured eyes, but it was only a flash and then the person suddenly disappeared, as though pulled violently back.

"It couldn't be!" Hatfield gasped.

For the face at the window was familiar. He believed that it was the face of Jay Rogers!

"I should've thought of this!" he muttered the next moment.

Hatfield was upset, startled by the glimpse he had had of Rogers. For the more he considered it, the more likely it became that the prisoner was his young friend.

"They're holdin' him here — mebbe beat him up some when they grabbed him," he decided. "Bane and Phelps are in it together. They got a big set-up, with all this money they're cheatin' folks out of. Rogers must have found out too much, and Phelps wanted him to quit goin' after Frenchie DeLuys. Wonder how Frenchie ties in with it all?"

One of the guards was bearing down on him, and he veered off, dragging along, back toward his tent.

'Mebbe they needed help, a strong-arm gang which DeLuys could furnish,' his thoughts ran on. 'These hombres doin' sentry duty got a tough look. S'pose DeLuys furnishes such, fellers who can be depended on not to call in the law? Bane's plainly a humbug, and from what little I've already seen, he's a lot worse! What's his game?'

He could deduce some of it. The Frontier Hospital, money from the deluded sick flocking to it, in answer to the publicity. Phelps came in handy, with the *Call*. He had come to Culverton ahead of Bane, to look over the town, prepare the way and hail the new 'doctor.'

'They used pore Rogers, fooled him, made him write that hogwash,' he mused.

He had brought his saddle and bags into the small tent which was just long enough to accommodate his body. The cot consisted of a rough wooden frame with ropes to hold the cornshuck ticking. The legs were only six inches high so that the sag with his weight let most of him rest on the ground.

From his tent, he watched the big ranchhouse. Dark was at hand, and several new guards went toward the building, disposing themselves about it, apparently going on duty for the night.

'Makes it harder, but I got to try and save Rogers,' thought the Ranger.

12

In the Night

DARK fell over the vast hinterland. Some candles and lanterns burned in the shacks and tents of Bane's victims. There were lights in the kitchen quarters, the office, and some other sections of the rambling main house. Hatfield could see the front of it.

He tried to figure the post and time of passing of the sentry in the drive, whose head he could see as the man went by the lighted windows. Awareness of Rogers' danger, a pressing urgency, was driving him on, aside from his desire to pin Bane and Phelps to the wall.

He removed his boots for they would scrape the pebbles, and make it difficult to move quietly. He substituted well-worn moccasins. His black hair he bound back out of the way with his kerchief and darkened his face and hands with dirt he scraped up, so there would be no sheen from his skin. He could not crawl wearing his cartridge belts, so he stowed spare shells here and there in his pockets, and carried only one Colt .45, thrust inside his shirt. Also he had his knife.

With too many people moving about, he had to wait another hour before he could start out. But the camp quieted down early, and the moon would not be up for a time.

The Ranger checked the immediate vicinity, found it clear. He snaked from his tent, and hastily fastened the flap behind him. Taking advantage of the land's contours, he crawled around until he could reach the comparative safety of a shrub clump fifty yards from the house. Checking the guards — there was one at the side he was on, another in front — he picked his next stopping place and made it without being spied.

The lighted, unbarred windows of the ranchhouse were open to the warm air. Now and then a patient — the wealthier ones evidently lived in the main structure — could be glimpsed. Feeling his way, Hatfield crouched in the black shadows of the trees skirting the driveway which curved its main section to the front entry and had a straight branch to the rear, for delivery of food and other supplies.

He had to wait for some time, to catch a few moments while the backs of both guards were turned. His moccasins made no sound as he flitted rapidly to the veranda, went over the rail, and froze in the darkness. Sounds came from inside, the sound of voices, and the tread of people moving about. He was ready to run or fight if he had to, but by careful timing and luck, he avoided being seen, and soon had an opportunity try the closed office door.

It was open. Phelps and Bane had gone in that way. The reception room was dark and nobody was in there. The door into Bane's sanctum stood ajar, and a lamp burned low on the desk. The light gleamed on the fat horsehair sofa, and caught the whitened bones of the skeleton suspended from the wall. The chemical odors assaulted his flared nostrils.

Hatfield stood in the outer room, as he checked up. The office seemed to be empty. He could hear many sounds in the big place, but none he could sift out as immediately threatening.

He kept low as he entered Bane's office, so he would not be spied from outside by the guard on that side. There was a closed door into the rear of Bane's private quarters. When he carefully tried this, he found it to be bolted from the other side.

'This is as far as I go thisaway,' he thought, chagrined at being unable to penetrate to the room in which he had glimpsed Jay Rogers.

He retired to the higher end of the black sofa, crouching there as he tried to decide on his next move. Should he go back to Culverton and, throwing what advantages he had gained to the winds, pick enough of a posse to rush the hospital and save Rogers?

But that did not appeal to him. Not only would he lose what he had won, but it might not be enough to save the reporter. If Bane and Phelps feared Rogers as a witness, they could kill him during the attack, before Hatfield and his friends could smash into the fortified section. And Bane probably had trail guards as well as gate sentries. He would have plenty of time to kill Rogers if he wished and escape.

A strange sound startled him, made his hackles rise.

'Sounds like dry bones rattlin'!' he thought.

It was exactly that. The skeleton, animated by exterior vibrations, was dancing at the end of its golden wire. Footsteps, murmurings, came to his keen ears just as he reached this conclusion. They were close at hand, in the rear of the office. Somebody was at that locked door, and a breath later metal rasped as a bolt was shot back.

Hatfield had a short interval in which he was able to snake in between the horsehair sofa and the wall, drawing up his long legs so that he was completely hidden. Then the inner door opened and men came into the office.

He could see three sets of feet by peeking under the low couch. One pair belonged to Counselor Phelps; the second to Dr. Bane, who was talking animatedly; the third set were cased in carpet slippers and the bottom of a blue dressing-gown was visible to the Ranger, who tried to still his breath which sounded like a steam engine to him.

"No, Mr. Mallory," Bane was saying suavely, "no finer, nobler cause can be found on earth than the alleviation of suffering. There are poor people who cannot afford medical attention and must suffer and die without it. You have no immediate family, as you have told me. The fortune you have made in mining could not be devoted to a more splendid work."

"I'm convinced now, Doc." The speaker was the owner of the thin ankles, ending in the carpet slippers. His voice was none too strong. "Yuh got a great place here, all right. I've enjoyed it and yuh've showed me lots of attention. I'm an old man and I ain't got too many more years to live. I'd like to think, like yuh say, that my money's bein' used to help pore folks. Was broke myself once, yuh savvy. I roamed the country thirty years before I struck the Last Chance Mine in the desert and hit her rich." The old miner coughed. "The sickness got me. Too much dust in them holes. But I'm a fighter, Doc, always was. I won't be one to give in to it."

"That's the spirit. Counselor, are you all ready for Mr. Mallory?"

"Yes, gentlemen," replied Phelps in his throaty voice.

Papers rustled. Bane sat on the edge of his desk, the miner in dressing-gown and slippers took a chair, and Hatfield could now see the thin white face and thin hair. It was the old man with whom he had seen Bane previously.

'Been workin' on him, I reckon,' he decided. 'Bane's talked him into willin' his money to the doc!'

A quill pen scratched in the silence, then the old miner, Mallory, said:

"I guess that's the last, ain't it, Counselor? I'm mighty tired tonight."

"That's the lot, sir," said Phelps.

Bane cleared his throat. "You'd better get right to bed, Mr. Mallory. Here, take this. It's your regular sleeping potion."

"Thanks, Doc," said Mallory. "That stuff yuh give me works mighty well. I sleep like a log — only next day I feel sort of washed out."

"You'll feel a good deal better tomorrow," said Bane.

Liquid gurgled. Phelps coughed, after a time.

"Say, it don't taste like the other, Doc," Mallory said. "Gets me in the throat!" His voice was strangling. "Ain't the same! What've yuh give me — " The weakening tones died off.

"That's done it," said Bane sharply. "Don't let him fall there, Phelps. Hold his arm. Here, we'll carry him to his room. Get hold of his arms. The old fool's dyin' already."

"His heart wasn't too strong at that," croaked Phelps, a sickly note in his voice. "Couldn't we have waited and let nature take her course?"

"Certainly not," snapped Bane. "The old goat might have strung it out for five or ten more years, and he could have changed his will any time. What if one of these flighty young women hooked him? Strychnin's much better. It'll look like he died in his sleep. We'll let Maria find him in the morning. Lend a hand — hurry."

Phelps grunted, for he found any sort of work distasteful. Bane was giving orders:

"You'd better write the obit tonight, Phelps, and lay it on thick, how the old fellow, grateful to the famous Dr. Bane who saved his life and made his last years joyful, left his entire fortune as an endowment to the Frontier Hospital."

"I just don't feel in the mood tonight, Bane. Why can't we have young Rogers do the writing? He'll handle it better than I."

"All right, if you can make him."

The skeleton danced as they moved through the rear hall.

With rage in his heart at Bane's coldblooded killing of a defenseless old man, the Ranger crept from behind the sofa. Bane had struck again. Hatfield could not save Mallory now. He chalked up another horrible deed against Bane. Going to the inner door, which they had left open as they carried Mallory away, he scanned the corridor. Several doors opened off it, and at the end was a wide, lighted entry into a back sitting room.

The skelelton jiggled and Hatfield shrank back. Bane and Phelps were returning. They paused before a door which Hatfield believed was the room in which he had glimpsed Rogers. Bane unlocked a padlock with a brass key on a chain.

"Rogers!" ordered Bane. "Come here."

Again behind the sofa, Hatfield saw a pair of bare feet — Jay Rogers' feet.

"How do you feel, my boy?" Phelps said, kindly enough. "Better tonight?"

"My head aches," muttered Rogers. "How long are you going to keep me here?"

"Oh, not much longer — a day or two perhaps," replied Phelps. Bane has agreed to give you one more chance if you'll travel with us."

"That's right, Rogers," said Bane, "but you'll have to prove it."

"I — I can't do it. What do you want with me now? I'd just managed to fall asleep,"

"I want you to do a little writing, Jay," said Phelps.

"I won't do it. I refuse to help you cheat anymore people, Bane."

"This isn't publicity, Jay," said Phelps quickly, as Bane growled a curse. "An old miner, Tige Mallory, has just died and he's left his money to the hospital. We want to write his obit. The *Call* comes out tomorrow, you know, and I've missed your assistance. I'm swamped with work."

"I won't do anything," said Rogers stubbornly.

He gave a sharp cry a moment later, and Hatfield heard a thud. Then Jay Rogers sprawled on the floor in front of Bane's desk. Hatfield saw that his face was swollen from cuts and bruises. He wore only a torn shirt and a pair of drawers. Bane crouched over him, and poised in his hand was a sharp scalpel with which he had jabbed Rogers.

"I'm sick of you, you young rat!" Bane cried angrily.

Hatfield's fingers reached his Colt stock. He would kill Bane, if need be, though he doubted if he could get out of the stockade alive, with Rogers on his hands. There were too many guards around, and the ruckus would fetch them all down on him.

"But Phelps intervened. "Please, Bane, don't. Let me talk to him. I'm sure he'll listen to reason . . . Jay, don't you realize that if you ever want to see Della again, you must act sensibly? Listen to me! I can write the obit if need be. You won't save anything or anybody by refusing. Certainly not yourself."

"Well — all right," Rogers replied shakily. "I don't suppose it makes any difference. But my head's awfully woozy, Phelps."

He seemed groggy, and his voice was weak. The Ranger wondered if Bane might not have been feeding him drugs, to keep him quiet. The stout Phelps held Rogers' arm as the reporter sat down at the desk, while Bane watched, sneering. There was a sadistic streak in Bane, and at the slightest prod his fierce, ungovernable temper flared to killing peak.

For a time a pen scratched, Phelps, reading over Rogers' shoulder, would make a suggestion now and again.

"Good, good stuff," said the counselor cheerily. "You see, Bane, I told you'd he'd prove useful."

Bane did not reply to this. The smell of his burning cheroot mingled with the druggy odors of the office.

When Rogers finished writing, Bane escorted him back to his room and the padlock was snapped on his door. Phelps waited in the office, and glass tinkled as the counselor poured himself a dose of his favorite 'medicine.'

Bane rejoined the man, sitting down by the desk. They drank and smoked together.

"How do you feel, Sam?" inquired Bane, after a time.

"I? Well enough, considering the strain. You know how I loathe violence."

"Lucky for us that I don't. We'd be in a pretty mess if I hadn't nerve enough to strike down an enemy at the proper moment. Now look. We're goin' to dispose of Rogers. He tried to signal a patient from his window today.

I've been feedin' him stuff to keep him quieted down and I can always say he's sick and has to be kept confined so he won't hurt himself. That takes care of any noises the folks happen to hear from this wing. But it can't go on forever. I won't have Rogers around any longer. He's too dangerous to us."

Phelps sighed heavily. "Ah, I'm sorry," he said. "I'd hoped the lad would see the light. I have a soft spot in my heart for Jay."

"No wonder, seein' as he does most of your work for you!" Bane was coarsely jovial. "You old hypocrite! You can pick up somebody else to do the needed writin' and run the paper, someone who'll work with us."

"Very well. However, I do like the boy. If only he wasn't such a jackass! By the way, Bane, I sounded out Thornton, and I'm afraid he won't listen to reason, either."

"I didn't think he would. What does he want for the big block of land between here and town?"

"A small fortune," answered Phelps. "He has inflated ideas of its value, due to the boom."

"We'll get rid of Thornton then, as well as Rogers. I'd like to get my hands on the Elite, along with his other properties. That place is a gold mine. As for the land, a number of people want to buy and build so as to be near the springs — and me! Besides, Thornton can't be fixed. You said so yourself. In the fall, you'll run for country sheriff, and you want full control of Culverton, so we can appoint a new city marshal friendly to us. It's the only way for us to be really safe here. Thornton's capable of raising the countryside against us, if he grows suspicious."

"You're perfectly right, Bane. How quickly do you think we can sell off the Thornton land?"

"We'll have all the time we need. We'll make it if we have to. The biggest single item yet is Mallory's money. You claim it'll take weeks to probate his will and get the cash."

"True, true. We must hold on until it's settled. I'll see to it myself, take the will along with me tonight."

"You'll go to work right away on it?"

"Yes, and I only hope there'll be no contest of the will," said Phelps. "If there is, it may delay us for a year."

Bane cursed, and poured himself another drink. "Then we can't absolutely count on the Mallory money. We'll squeeze out every two-bit piece in sight, however, and we ought to be well-fixed."

Hatfield's legs, drawn up to keep them from sight across the room, ached with cramps. Bane and his tool, the nervous, flabby Phelps conferred and drank, and the time dragged endlessly for the Ranger, unable to move a muscle in the little space behind the bulging horsehair sofa. Interesting as the information was that he was obtaining, he was in agony. Only his steel will kept him from shifting, giving himself away.

But Hatfield knew that he could not hold out for much longer.

13

Evil Plans

PLENTY of drinks were necessary to mellow the ferocious Bane, and loosen his tongue. But he had them now.

"Sam," he said, a bit thickly, "we've worked together a long while, haven't we? You're a good fellow, one I can depend on, even thought you have weak points. But — well, I too, have 'em, those weak spots. I guess everybody does."

"You — what?" asked Phelps thickly.

"I don't feel as sure of myself, as comfortable as I ought to, with everything goin' so well," confessed Bane.

"How so?"

"Well, there's aways the chance of a slip. Like that accursed Army major chancin' to pass through and recognize me. I've had a funny feeling lately. Hard to say just what it is, but I have it now."

"Such as what?" Phelps was steeped in whiskey.

"As though somebody was watching me, dogging me! I keep tellin' myself it's nerves, Sam. But I didn't like the business of DeLuys being arrested. We had to go to a lot of fuss to rescue Frenchie or he'd have turned on us. You can trust a man of DeLuys' caliber just so far. If you don't back him up, he's liable to expose you. Who in tarnation blazes downed Frenchie that night in Culverton?"

"I've wonderd about that myself," said Phelps. "Rogers was on the spot, and he's a good reporter, but he couldn't say who it was. He claimed that someone gunned Frenchie's men, but he had only a glimpse of a man firing from the shadows."

"Was Rogers telling the truth?"

"I'm not entirely sure, Bane. He's

not a very good liar."

"From all I've been able to learn," went on Bane, "the fellow who butted in on both the Anson and Spear hold-ups was an unusually large man. That's one thing the excited men agree on. Did you see Rogers with any big strangers around the town?"

Phelps was thinking. Then he answered:

"Only Jim Hart, the big donkey I sent here, Bane, and he'd be incapable of such terrific fighting power as the mysterious stranger displayed. All Hart can think of is his own ills. Isn't he comical? I hope you enjoyed the note I sent by him! He can't read his own name, and he's sure he met Will Shakespeare selling his own works!"

Phelps laughed heartily, and Bane joined in.

Bane was keen, mused the hidden Ranger. He had sensed the presence of a formidable enemy, the Texas Ranger who had come to Culverton on the killer's trail.

Then Bane, his laugh subsiding, was speaking again.

"Why don't you look around town tomorrow, Phelps? it is possible that Rogers has a connection we can check. I don't want to leave any loop-holes. Have you looked over Rogers' effects? He may have kept papers or a diary which would tell us something vital."

"Perhaps. I'll go in the morning, and look over his things. The landlady's a simple-minded old thing. She'll let me in, and I'll tell her that I had a secret message from Rogers to ship his belongings to him."

A chair creaked. "I must be on my way, Bane." The fat counselor yawned. "Old Dobbin will take me home. He knows the way. I'll be up again tomorrow. Good luck."

"Good luck is all we need," said Bane, wait . . . There's someone at the porch door."

Bane glided through the reception room and voices murmured outside.

"Who is it?" called Phelps.

"It's Frenchie. He's comin' in. I'll let him take Rogers out with him tonight."

The counselor clucked nervously. "If it's all the same to you, Bane, I'll be going. You won't need me anymore this evening?"

"No. Go on home and get some sleep, Sam."

The two went to the veranda door, and Hatfield could snatch a few moments in which to shift his position and stretch his tortured leg muscles, without the chance of being detected. It was sheer luxury to move, even a little, and he dared to breathe deeply again. His left shoulder had gone to sleep, and prickled violently as the blood returned to the veins.

Booted feet, with big Mexican spurs tinkling, followed the wiry little Bane's into the office.

"I wasn't expecting you tonight, Frenchie," said Bane, "but I'm glad you've come." Glass tinkled. "Help yourself."

"Obliged, Doc. Don't mind if I do."

DeLuys sprawled in the chair which Phelps had recently vacated. The counselor was on his way back to the hotel where he dwelt in Culverton.

"There are several things I wanted to say," began Bane. "But first, what brings you here? Nothing wrong, I hope?"

"No, suh, not at all. We picked up a hundred head of beefs and the boys'll drive 'em to the slaughterin' pens down by the crik before sunup. Yuh're runnin' short, so Jason sent me word. Yuh got a lot of mouths to feed here, Doc."

"True. Jason takes care of the commissary division. Where did you get these cows?"

"Some from Anson's Double A, others from the Bar Two and KL. They're all prime animals. Melt in yore mouth."

"How about the brands? Suppose someone recognized them in our pens?"

DeLuys laughed. "Don't let that worry you, Doc. We pick off a few here and there, collect 'em. We burn off the brands soon as we run 'em to our secret corral in the woods. When they're slaughtered we bury the hides. It's a cinch, if yuh savvy yore business."

'They make money at both ends and in the middle,' thought the Ranger. 'Bane even feeds his victims on stolen beef!'

A drawer squeaked as Bane pulled it open in his desk.

"I have some money for you, Frenchie . . . You know Jay Rogers, the *Call* reporter who worked up the case against you? A dangerous witness, if ever you happen to be arrested again. Well, I have Rogers here. I want you to take him out and dispose of him in some safe place. No fuss, understand? It can't be near the hospital. I want no disturbance around the grounds."

"It'll be a cinch, Doc. Glad yuh got Rogers. He could testify agin me!"

Frenchie rubbed his bronzed throat which was banded by a red kerchief with yellow polka-dots. "We'll take care of Rogers. I got three men ridin' with me this evenin'. I want to see Jason for a few minutes before I leave. Others, except for my camp guards in the monte, are fetchin' in the steers."

"Rogers' hash is settled, then. Now listen carefully to this. I want Vance Thornton out of the way. He's a nuisance, and a menace to us all. He can't be bought. He's a leader in these parts, liable to rouse the countryside if he grows suspicious. But I want this job done carefully, too. No crude stuff. Catch Thornton at night, alone, and spirit him away. I don't want anymore of these knock-down-drag-out scraps in the town."

"All right, Boss. I been lyin' low like yuh told me to. Though sometimes I hone for a real spree."

"Before long you can enjoy all you want, Frenchie. When Thornton's out of the way, and Counselor Phelps is elected sheriff, we'll run things as we like. You and your boys can help Phelps win the next election. You should be able to garner quite a few votes."

"Oh, shore." DeLuys nodded. "I run an election on the Border one time and savvy how to do it. Thing is to count the votes before anybody else does. Then yuh can add what yuh need to elect yore choice!"

"Good. Now, it's getting late. We'll get Rogers and you can run him out." Bane rose, saying, "You have three men with you?"

"Yes, suh. That's right."

"Have them come in and give a hand."

DeLuys nodded. "In a jiffy, Doc. But before I go, I want to tell yuh what a pleasure it is to work for an hombre like you. You got real brains, boss, and I'm shore glad I hooked up with yuh."

"Glad you feel that way, Frenchie. Stick along and you'll see that we'll own Texas before long."

"I believe it," said DeLuys.

Frenchie went to the front. More booted legs showed to the watching Ranger. They trailed Bane down the back hall and a lock clicked. Faint sounds reached Hatfield and soon DeLuys and his men returned, passing through the office, carrying a limp form wrapped in a brown blanket.

"So long, Doc," said Frenchie. "I'll take care of everything."

Bane saw them out the front way. Soon he walked, with his catlike tread, through the office, shooting the bolts on the doors, He had a last drink at his desk and turned out the office lamp. Hatfield heard a third bolt, the one at the corridor, slide home. Bane's receding tread died off in the rear.

Hatfield got up and stretched himself. He tiptoed to the front and worked back the bolt, entering the dark reception room. The porch door was before him and that bolt, too, responded to the long, sensitive fingers. He opened the

183

door just a crack and peeked out.

Phelps had driven his slow rig out. DeLuys' three men, one carrying Rogers slung across his horse, were moving to the gate, where a lantern gleamed in the night. The moon was up, bathing the world in a silver light, but the shadows were black. Frenchie had gone around to the rear quarters to see his friend Jason.

A guard paced the gravel driveway. Hatfield had to be cautious, watch and wait for his chance to open the porch door enough to slip through. On hands and knees, he made the railing. When the right moment came, he slipped over, dropped to earth, and reached the first line of bushes.

Vague sounds, of sleeping humanity, of creatures stirring in the night, the soft rustle of last year's dried seed pods and grass, of birds and insects, filled the warm air.

"I got to save Rogers!" he told himself grimly. "This is the last chance!"

It was an impossibility to rush the guarded main gate on a horse. Barbed wire fence surrounded the grounds and Goldy was in a corral not far from the rear of the service quarters, to which Frenchie DeLuys had just gone to see Jason, the butcher. There were lights back there, and armed sentries to watch that area and the corral in which the horses were kept.

"I'll have to leave him and run for it," decided Hatfield.

He could not take a chance of being caught as he tried to snake the sorrel out. Even if Goldy kept quiet, the other horses would be sure to make a fuss. Besides he would need to cut through the three-strand triple wire to make a hole for his horse to pass through, and then he would have to seek a trail which Goldy could negotiate in the night.

His decision made, the Ranger was already turning, on his way to the limits of the enclosure. Bush, trees, contours of the ground, hid the crouched figure

185

of the officer as he snaked up to the fence. He managed to prop up the lowest strand and went under on his back. The wire hummed, but the faint sound did not cause an alarm. He crawled toward a patch of dark pines up the hillside. He had come out on the east side of the Frontier Hospital, and as soon as he had made the rise beyond the trees, he got up and began to run.

His moccasins came in handy now. He could never have made it in heavy, spurred boots. Light as an Indian on his feet, the tall Ranger headed through the hills for the road which led to Culverton.

"I got to make it!" he told himself, over and over. "It's Rogers' last chance!"

14

A Buggy Ride

SWIFTLY Jim Hatfield climbed the heights, shortcutting afoot. The road had to skirt this elevation, and he counted on the slowness of old Dobbin, Counselor Phelps' carriage horse. On Hatfield alone depended all — Roger's life, Thornton's life, and that of others. On the Ranger was the burden of smashing Bane's rapidly growing power.

He had to chance a misstep, a fall, as he sped over the rough ground, skirting rock upthrusts and the patches of woods that blocked him. He ran at his best speed, and the air whistled past his ears. His breath began to rasp in his throat, and the sweat poured from his big body, ran down his face, cutting runnels in the dirt he had smeared on his skin. His fists were clenched and his rugged mouth was set.

Thorned branches clutched at him in spots, tore his clothing, scratched him till the blood ran. A whiplike branch he had not seen in the shadowed light slashed at his face, cut his cheek and the bridge of his nose. Once his ankle turned under him, as a loose stone rolled under his swiftly moving foot.

Suddenly he broke from low brush onto the dirt road which wound around the mountain, the road from which Bane's lane branched. He drew back, crouching at the side of the highway. The air he drew into his heavy lungs burned his throat and he was drenched with perspiration.

"Have I made it?" he thought.

Perhaps old Dobbin had already passed this point, though he didn't think the slow horse could have come this far in such a short time. He had to rest, in any case.

Culverton lay some distance off, in the river valley. Hatfield waited, straining his ears, regaining his wind. After a while his breathing quieted. He wiped his face with his shirt tail, then smeared more dirt on his features to kill any sheen.

The moon, nearly full, was well up in the sky and its light streaked the earth. In open spaces, a man could see for a good distance, but shadows were black.

"'Dog it, he must have got by me!' he mused, squatting in the brush by the dirt way. 'I'll have to run all the way to town — and I'll miss DeLuys and Rogers shore!'

A faint sound, a light wheel squeaking a bit as it rolled, caught at his straining attention. He made ready, listening for it again. Then he saw the buggy's dark shape on the stretch of road visible, slowly approaching. Old Dobbin never ran if he could get out of it. He walked, rather majestically, as a proud old man might. He knew the way home, back to his own stable, where he was petted and fed.

Fifty yards from the spot where the Ranger crouched, Dobbin stopped, and turned to pluck at a particularly appetizing leafy shrub which grew at the edge of the road. He tore off a couple of mouthfuls and slowly masticated, resting and enjoying a bite at the same time before resuming his slow journey home. The driver of the buggy made no objection.

'Why the old rascal must be asleep over the reins!' thought the Ranger.

It was so. Counselor Phelps, slouched back in the two-seated buggy, with its patent-leather top up, was snoring, overcome by natural weariness plus the large amount of whisky — or 'medicine' — he had consumed.

Dobbin finished his snack and walked on. When he came to the point where the tall Ranger waited, Dobbin scented and saw the man but he did not shy or raise any objections. He had long since given up arguing and fighting humans over their queer notions. Not even a gunshot close to his ear would make

Dobbin buck any more. He would only draw himself up and look injured.

It was simple for the lithe Hatfield to leap into the slowly moving buggy, from the left side, he sat down, squeezing in beside Phelps, who was sprawled in the seat.

"Huh?" gruntd the counselor, hardly waking up. "Are — are we home, Dobbin?"

He was not yet roused. He grumbled and moaned, stirring, but leaning back and seeking to resume his interrupted sleep.

Hatfield seized the reins and tried to turn Dobbin, who for the first time objected strenuously. Dobbin wished to go on home to the stable, but after a few jerks on the leather straps, he gave up and swung in the road, the buggy creaking, the wheel rubbing the low side of the body as the vehicle made the sharp turn.

"Uh-uh!" Phelps cleared his throat.

He opened his eyes, and pushed heavily against Hatfield.

At last he was coming out of his drunken stupor, and suddenly realized that someone was sitting beside him.

"Who's that?" he demanded, a quaver in his voice: "Who are you? Where am I?"

"I'm Jim Hart, Counselor. And we're goin' for a buggy ride."

"Hart — Jim Hart?" repeated the counselor, regaining his aplomb. He peered at the tall fellow snugged in the buggy seat. "Why, so it is! How in heavens' name did you get here in the buggy, beside me? I thought you were taking the baths at Dr. Bane's, my boy."

"I was."

Hatfield was urging Dobbin on now. The old gelding turned around to look at him, astounded that he should be asked to run, and uphill, at that.

"You — you got in the buggy, to take me home, see me safe to my quarters, I suppose? It isn't necessary, Hart." Phelps was completely at sea and was probing for information. "But we're going the wrong way to reach Culverton, you know."

"I savvy. We ain't goin' to Culverton — not yet, Phelps. First we're goin' to try and save Jay Rogers' life. As yuh know, Frenchie DeLuys has him and means to kill him when he gets him into the monte."

The counselor's breath drew sharply into his lungs.

W-what's that?"

Hatfield could feel the soft, fat flesh pressed to his side begin to shake. Goose pimples covered the counselor. "Yuh heard what I said, Phelps. Yuh was in Bane's office tonight, just like I was."

"You! You were there?" The counselor's brained reeled. He could not believe what he heard.

"Hid behind that bulky black sofa Bane used to lay his victims on."

"You — must have heard some interesting talk, then?"

"Oh, shore. All of it. Bane's a root-toot-tootin' devil, ain't he? I mean, lucky for you and him he don't balk at little matters like killin' Army doctors, wealthy patients, and orderin' Rogers, Thornton and others done in and so on. HG's got fine plans."

Phelps was groaning. "You fooled me — very skillfully, my boy. Hart — if that's your name — you *can* read, I suppose?"

"Yes, suh. I studied enineerin' two years in college. We had to do a lot of readin' then. Includin' Shakespeare. Comes in handy, knowin' such things, don't it? Like tonight. My gelding is in the hospital corrals and I couldn't shake him out with me. Remember in King Richard the Third when he said, 'A hoss, a hoss, my kingdom for a hoss!' He meant it, and so did I. Dobbin's the best I could do."

Phelps was silent for a time. Dobbin was straining to reach the top of the grade so he might coast for a spell.

"You're the big man who interfered and saved Amson and Spear," declared the counselor. "I'd never have believed it. A clever impersonation you gave when you tricked me into giving you the letter to Bane." He was feeling his way, trying to find what the game was.

"I had to get inside for a close look at Bane and his set-up," explained the Ranger gently, his voice soft, polite. "Yuh see, I come to Culverton on official business. I'm a Texas Ranger, name of Hatfield."

Phelps' start was telegraphed through the flabby body pressed to Hatfield's side. The counselor's gasp was sheer panic.

"A — Texas Ranger!"

"We had reports of trouble over this way, after you and Bane arrived. Killin's, complaints and so on. No, yuh don't!"

It was easy to throw a hand over and grip Phelps' fat wrist. Inside the frock coat was a holster holding a short-barreled pistol. The Ranger's fingers closed on the counselor's wrist and the bone cracked in its socket. Phelps uttered a squeal of pain.

"Don't — don't hit me, Ranger!" he begged.

"I'm surprised at yuh, Counselor," drawled Hatfield, "tryin' anything as crude as that! I thought yuh hated violence so much and here yuh are, tryin' to start a real, old-fashioned brawl with me! Figgered yuh'd listen to reason, to save yore own precious hide."

"I will! Don't shoot me. Please, let go of my wrist. You're breaking it." Phelps was gasping, in fear and pain.

"I will, soon as I get that gun."

He slipped the pistol from its pouch, and placed it under his foot, on the buggy floor. Phelps sat rigid as Hatfield patted around to see if the counselor had any more weapons, but that was all Phelps carried.

"What do you intend to do with me, sir?" inquired Phelps, as Dobbin reached the crest of the rise and the buggy rattled down the slope toward the next hill. His teeth chattered in his head, his lax lips gleamed.

"Well, yuh savvy yuh're just as much of a rascal as Bane, in yore way, Phelps," said the Ranger. "But yuh ain't killed anybody that I know of. I might see yuh got off with prison if yuh helped me pin Doc Bane. And there are a couple little things to do tonight. Such as seein' can we save Jay Rogers from DeLuys."

"Rogers — DeLuys? No, you're mad You can't do that! You're alone, except for me, that is. I can't help. Frenchie has a large band of savage fighting men with him."

"Most of 'em are drivin' in steers or back at camp. Frenchie and only three hombres are runnin' Rogers into the bush to kill him. I couldn't get near enough, myself, to save Jay, because Frenchie'd prob'ly shoot him before I could snatch Rogers from him. DeLuys savvies that Jay'll testify agin him. However, Frenchie is a friend of yores and he'll let yuh come up close — with me sort of mooched down on the seat beside yuh."

Phelps' teeth began to rattle like castanets. He had a vivid imagination.

"But — when they open fire, they may hit me — us!" he protested. He thought of another loophole. "Old Dobbin can never overtake the mustangs they're ridin', Ranger!"

"There's a fair chance. DeLuys went around to chew the fat with Jason, Bane's butcher, over them stolen cows. We ain't far from the hospital turn-in. Are yuh with me — or agin me?"

The Ranger's fingers vised again on Phelps' wrist.

"With you, of course! What do you want me to do?"

"Hail DeLuys when he comes long. Get the buggy in close to the group. There'll be four of 'em, and one's got Jay Rogers tied behind him. Then all yuh have to do is duck and save yore skin in case anything happens."

Phelps groaned. He wrung his hands. "I'm not built for such work, Ranger — really I'm not."

But he could not refuse. He feared

the big man with the terrible grip, the glinting, strong eyes, the masterful voice.

"Don't forget, Counselor," warned Hatfield. "I'm settin' right beside yuh. If yuh should be foolish enough to try and warn Frenchie, or interfere with me, the first shot goes for you. No matter what, savvy?"

"I — savvy."

"Yuh know where the corral is that DeLuys runs them stolen beeves to, down by the crik?"

"Yes," replied Phelps, his voice sickly. "There's another path to it, from the west, out of the woods."

"Then we ain't likely to bump into Frenchie's main gang . . . Easy, now, here comes some riders on the lane from Bane's!"

The moonlight, as Hatfield had turned the buggy, was on Phelps' side. The man stopped the horse with ease, for Dobbin was always happy to stop and rest.

On the road from Bane's Frontier

Hospital, horsemen loomed against the sky. Hatfield counted four of them. They saw the buggy and slowed, then came on, pushing their mustangs.

It was Frenchie DeLuys and his outlaws. A blanket-swathed figure lay across one of the horses. Jay Rogers!

15

Outlaw End

GRIPPING his Colt, with its hammer spur back under his thumb, Hatfield slouched down in the buggy seat, shadowed by the fat Phelps, who was trembling like a leaf in the wind.

"Hey, there, Phelps, is that you?" sang out DeLuys.

The bandit chieftain was surprised to see the counselor's buggy, which he knew well.

"Answer him — say yuh got a busted wheel," whispered the Ranger, prodding Phelps.

"Yes, Frenchie," replied Phelps. His voice was shaking. "A wheel — it's broken. I've just been sitting here waiting."

Hombre, yuh're shore in a tight,

ain't yuh?" said DeLuys, his white teeth gleaming as he rode up to the buggy side.

The outlaw believed that Phelps was so under the influence of liquor that he could not speak properly. But as he swung his dark-hided mustang so as to face the counselor, he glimpsed the bulk of Hatfield's figure, slumped at Phelps' side.

"Who in blazes is that, Phelps? I didn't savvy yuh had anybody with yuh!"

DeLuys' three men had come up, and sat their horses, close to their chief. They were off guard, for Sam Phelps was a friend, an important assistant to Jonathan Bane, the boss.

"He's a — it's a — " began Phelps, but his voice broke, and the sentence ended in a squeak of terror.

Suspicion streaking through his startled senses, DeLuys dropped his left hand to his Colt handle, his bunched leather chaps pushing the holster up as he straddled his horse. But the bandit froze on the instant, for he was staring into Hatfield's gun muzzle.

"Reach high, Frenchie!" the Ranger snapped.

Hatfield did not want to kill Frenchie DeLuys if he could help it. He would rather capture the fellow alive, and use him against Bane.

"What the devil!" snarled DeLuys. "Phelps, you fix this here trap? What kind of game is it?"

"I want Jay Rogers, Frenchie," Hatfield said smoothly.

DeLuys knew the danger of a pointed, steady pistol; he was only a few feet from Hatfield and in the moonlight in the rear of the buggy the Ranger Colt barrel gleamed. His men did not dare act, without some sign that their chief would fight, for it would mean his instant death. They waited for Frenchie to call the turn.

A long moment ticked off in eternity.

"Yuh got Rogers bundled on that hoss, DeLuys," Hatfield said. "Order yore man to untie him."

"Rogers is dead, mister," DeLuys growled.

A streak of dismay hit the Ranger and the muscles of his rugged face went taut. That might be so. DeLuys could have despatched the reporter with a knife, if not with a single shot through the brain. The main road was half a mile out from the Frontier Hospital, and a pistol report would scarcely be heard against the south wind. Even if heard, it would cause no alarm at such a distance.

"For yore own sake, Frenchie, I hope yuh're lyin'," drawled the Ranger. "Have yore man drop the body, or whatever's left of Rogers." As DeLuys still did not give the command, a sharp note entered his voice. "Pronto, yuh cussed hossthief! I ain't foolin'!"

"Oh, please, Frenchie, obey him!" gasped Phelps, finding his voice. "Let him have what he wants. He — he's a Texas Ranger!"

"Ranger!" DeLuys swayed in his

saddle, A bandit gave a quick, nervous curse.

Through the rear buggy window, the streak of moonlight struck the big man's cheek, and his gray-green eyes had darkened. They gleamed as they fixed Frenchie DeLuys. The Colt muzzle never wavered.

"Dan," ordered DeLuys, "cut that rope and let Rogers drop."

"Do it careful, Danny," said the Ranger. "Don't get any cute notions in yore little head."

These outlaws were fierce fighters and cold-blooded killers, but Jim Hatfield held them with a single Colt, for they sensed the powerful and determined personality behind the gun. He felt the tension, and was aware that DeLuys was obeying only from expediency, hanging on and watching for a chance to strike.

In order to rescue Jay Rogers, Hatfield had been forced to discard many advantages in the fight against Bane and his crew. He could never take the quartet and Phelps' rig with Rogers into town. The run was too long for that in the night. All he hoped for was to save Rogers — and now he wasn't certain whether Rogers was alive or not.

The Ranger could just glimpse the bandit, Danny, as the man stiffly dismounted, moving with slow motion so that none of his actions might be misconstrued. He loosened the lashings which held the blanket-swathed bundle on the mustang, and then lifted Rogers to the ground.

"Put him in here, beside the counselor and me," directed the Ranger.

Danny hesitated and glanced at DeLuys.

Do as he says, Danny," DeLuys grunted.

The outlaw hefted Rogers and moved to the buggy and this brought him between Hatfield and Frenchie. It was the chance DeLuys had been watching for, and he struck instantly. He made a fast draw, shielded by Dan's head and shoulders. It was completed in a second fraction, even with Frenchie's hands traveling from shoulder height as he had raised them. Guns flamed in the night, as DeLuys made his left-handed stab.

"No, no! Stop!" Counselor Phelps screeched.

The Ranger Colt exploded. The steady hand never wavered. The slug caught DeLuys above his left ear as he had spurred his black mustang around. The outlaw's pistol went off, but it was still canted downward, and Danny, Frenchie's own man, pitched forward with Rogers still in his arms. Danny fell against the buggy wheel, and Rogers landed on top of him.

Phelps scrunched down in the seat, sobbing with terror. There were two outlaws left after DeLuys collapsed in his saddle. As his horse nervously shied at the explosions and spurts of fire from the Colts, he went off on one side. But his foot was caught in the stirrup. The mustang moved off and then came to a stop, with the heavy drag of Frenchie's weight holding him.

The action had consumed but seconds, then Hatfield had thrown himself past Phelps, to deal with the remaining pair of outlaws.

The bandit in front, a cadaverous-faced man with a narrow unshaven face, got off a shot, but his horse was dancing and spoiled his aim. The bullet tore through the buggy top, and the counselor screamed as he heard the sound of its passing.

"I'm hit — I'm killed," he cried.

Hatfield was on the road, crouched in front of the jumbled heap that was Rogers and Danny. Danny's horse stood, his reins down, though he kicked and shied as had the other mustangs. Old Dobbin only shivered his hide and looked around inquiring. He was too tired from the run uphill to move.

The Ranger hastily threw a slug into the narrow-faced outlaw's shoulder, which stopped him and drove the fight out of him. He was swinging his

Colt to deal with the second when the fellow uttered a sharp cry and reached for the sky.

"Don't shoot! I quit!"

The Ranger Colt stared up at the pair, the one with the smashed shoulder, the stouter, round-faced one who had lost his nerve at the deadly fighting power of Jim Hatfield.

"Get down then, both of yuh. Turn yore backs and keep reachin'."

"I can't move my cussed shoulder," whined the wounded man.

"Well elevate yore left and turn round. I want to defang both of yuh before yuh get any more ideas."

"Ow-w!" The injured fellow cried out in pain as he slid off his saddle and obeyed the Ranger's orders. "This is killin' me! I can't stand it."

"Too bad Doc Bane ain't here to treat yuh," said Hatfield. "It's only what yuh deserve."

Counselor Phelps was completely sobered by shock and fear.

"Get down, Phelps," Hatfield said

impatiently, as Phelps kept on moaning. "You ain't hurt. C'mon — there's plenty of work to be done."

He removed the pistols from the spare holsters of the captives, and confiscated their knives, checking up to make sure they were entirely disarmed. Sometimes such professionals carried as many as four pistols, having a brace hidden under the clothing.

Phelps obeyed, groaning. He had to support himself for a time by holding onto the buggy wheel.

"I — I can't move, Ranger," he said weakly.

"C'mon — I want yuh to tie their hands behind 'em, Phelps," ordered Hatfield. "Lift Rogers into the buggy and prop him, on the seat . . . Is he still alive and kickin'?"

Watching the two men with their backs turned to him, the Ranger felt Rogers' face. It was hot, and the reporter was still breathing. Relief flooded through him. Rogers wasn't dead as DeLuys had said, no doubt trying to throw Hatfield off.

"I can't move a muscle," wailed Phelps.

Hatfield straightened up. His foot rose in a short arc, as he kicked Phelps where it would do the most good. It lifted the fat counselor an inch off the ground and hurt the Ranger's foot, cased only in a moccasin, but it was worth it, for Phelps went to work with alacrity.

Phelps hoisted Rogers to the buggy seat, and secured the hands of the two prisoners behind them. The wounded man screamed with pain as his arm was jerked around. Then, under Hatfield's direction, Phelps brought Danny's mustang. He was tamer than the usual Texas horse, and permitted Danny and DeLuys to be tied over his back.

Hatfield then had Phelps fastened the reins to the rear of the buggy. He had the wounded bandit climb in beside Phelps and the still unconscious Rogers — a tight squeeze. The fourth mounted at Hatfield's command, and the spare horse was fastened to his saddle-horn by a lariat, while the Ranger took Frenchie's fine black animal.

"You go first, Counselor," commanded the Ranger. "Dobbin savvies the way and it's mostly downhill. You next, feller. I'm ridin' in the rear, and I'll be all ready in case of a fuss. Move!"

The strange cavalcade proceded toward Culverton, under the silver moon.

'I was mighty lucky,' mused Hatfield.

As he fixed a quirly with one hand, his sharp eyes were observing the enemies he had taken. He was not thinking of the fight, in which he had downed DeLuys and winged another outlaw. But he was glad that none had escaped, to carry the alarm to Bane.

'I'll go through with it, and catch him right,' he thought. 'Also Frenchie's got a big bunch of gunnies back there in the monte and they can't be left to run loose.'

The time was speeding by. Dobbin moved slowly for he could be hurried just so much.

It was nearly two A.M. when the Ranger had Phelps pull up at the side of the Elite. The town was dark. The salons had closed for the night.

"We'll all go in together, fellers," said the Ranger.

Phelps led the way with dragging steps as they trooped into the hotel. The front door was unlocked, and the Ranger banged on the call bell at the desk. An oil lamp, turned down, hung in a wall bracket at the rear stairs which led to the upper rooms.

After a time, big Vance Thornton came down the steps, swearing and rubbing his sleepy eyes. He had pulled on his pants, but his feet and torso were bare.

"What in tarnation blazes is goin' on here this time of night!" he growled, as he saw the shadowy figures at the desk.

"It's me, Jim Hart — Hatfield, really,

213

Thornton. I got Frenchie DeLuys' remains outside, and I fetched in some prisoners. To say nothin' of Jay Rogers. They been holdin' him up at Bane's place and they were goin' to kill him."

"What's that — huh! Yuh got Rogers — and DeLuys!"

Thornton began swearing in a new vein, one of amazement. He hastily scratched a match and stared at the hangdog faces of Counselor Phelps and the two outlaws. The match burned his thumb and he quickly dropped it, and struck another. This time he touched it to the wick of the desk lamp, and the light came up.

"I ain't got too much time, Thornton," explained the Ranger. "I got to be moseyin' on back. Yuh better go fetched Marshal Tate and let him handle the prisoner end. Then I'd like to talk with yuh for a jiffy. I'll hold 'em here till yuh get back with Tate."

"Right, right! But how'd yuh do it?

What's Phelps got to do with it? Can I tell Dell that Rogers didn't run away, after all?"

"One at a time, Thornton. You bring the marshal and then we'll palaver."

16

New Allies

VANCE THORNTON galloped out, pausing to stare at the limp Rogers, still in the carriage, and at the dead men on the mustang tied to the buggy. Dobbin was asleep on his feet, his head down.

It was ten minutes before the hotel man returned with Zeke Tate. They carried Jay Rogers in and laid him on the couch at the side of the room. The amazed marshal stared at the tall, imperturbable Ranger, whose face was still streaked with dirt, whose head was bound with his kerchief, and on whose feet were moccasins.

"By Jupe, I don't savvy how yuh done it, Hart — but yuh have!" the town officer said at last. "Yuh got DeLuys and three of his men, and brought Rogers back, with on'y Phelps to help you?"

"Leave out Phelps or add him to the opposition," drawled the Ranger. "He's been in cahoots with DeLuys, and Doc Bane, who's the real enemy, all through, Tate. My right handle is Jim Hatfield, and I'm a Texas Ranger, come here to settle this trouble.

From a secret pocket, snugged under his shirt, Hatfield brought his Ranger star, the silver star on the silver circle which was the emblem of his great organization.

"A Ranger!" exclaimed Tate. "Cuss it, why didn't yuh tell me first off?"

"I like to get in and look over a place, before I start workin'."

Tate nodded. "Mebbe it pays, at that! Seein' what yuh done tonight!"

A slim figure in a blue robe, and with golden hair hanging in tight braids down her back, appeared from the stairs.

"Father!" a girl's voice called anxiously. "Are you all right? I heard

217

the noise. What's going on ?"

"Come here, Dell — come here, pronto!" called the excited Thornton. "Jay Rogers is back!"

Della Thornton came hesitantly forward.

"Where is he?" she asked. "What has he to say?" Then she saw Rogers' limp figure stretched on the couch. "Is he dead?" she whispered.

"No ma'am," the Ranger told her. "He's banged up some and he needs care and nursin'. He didn't run away, like we thought. He was took pris'ner by a passel of dirty outlaws. That note addressed to you wasn't written by Jay, but by this old scalawag Phelps."

Dell sped to Jay Rogers and knelt beside him.

"Jail's still got a hole in the wall, where they rescued Frenchie," remarked Tate.

"It'll be better if we keep the prisoners hid for a day or two, anyways," said the Ranger. " I reckon Thornton's got a storeroom where we can lock 'em under guard. Let's finish up. I got to talk to you boys before I pull out again."

With the marshal's and Thornton's aid, Hatfield quickly disposed of the captives. The bodies were taken to the stable, and would be buried quietly in Boot Hill. Tate would attend to that. Hatfield spoke with Thornton and Zeke Tate, when they had finished their tasks.

"All right," said Vance Thornton when he had been apprised of Phelps' and Bane's true status. "We're with yuh, Ranger, right to the hilt. Where yuh figger on goin' next?"

"Back to Bane's, before they find out I'm on the prowl," replied the Ranger. "You boys do like I said, and I'll meet yuh on the road tomorrer at noon."

On DeLuys' horse, the tall officer rode out of Culverton, hurrying to return to Bane's hospital. Near the spot where he had intercepted Counselor Phelps earlier in the night, Hatfield turned off into the bush and dismounted. He tethered the mustang on a long rope so the horse could graze.

"I'll send back for yuh tomorrer, boy," he said. "Yuh're too good an animal to work for outlaws."

He walked the rest of the way back to the barbed wire fence. The hospital was quiet in the small hours. There was a suspicious grayness, the false dawn, in the sky, as he crept under the wire. He made a cautious way toward his tent, only pausing to rub the smears from his face and hands at the edge of a spring, and to wash up.

His head had scarcely touched his saddle when he was asleep, for he was done in, run to a frazzle. He had won the first round in his fight against Jonathan Bane, and had won the support of Thornton and Tate in the battle.

The bright sunlight of the morning, the stirrings of people about him, awoke Hatfield. The few hours' nap had refreshed him, and he felt as hungry as a bear. He finished cleaning himself up and, pulling on his boots, hurried over to the dining pavilion, arriving just in time to enjoy a late and hearty breakfast.

When he had finished eating he rolled a smoke, and repaired to the corral down the way. En route, he saw a heavy-set man, with brown hair and a round head, and wearing a white apron, busily working at cutting up a hung steer. It was Jason, the hospital butcher.

"'Mornin', cowboy," sang out Jason. "Where you bound?"

"Oh, I figger I'll get out and ride to town on business, mister."

He went to the corral, and Goldy sighted him. The sorrel whinnied, and came trotting to nuzzle his hand. He smoothed the mount's arched neck with expert touch, and whispered:

"We're goin' to work now, Goldy."

Saddling up, he mounted and rode toward the front of the hospital. There were guards at the gate, as usual.

"Reckon I better set their minds at rest, before I leave," he decided, stopped in the driveway, dropped his reins, and entered the office.

The young woman attendant was at her desk. The connecting door into the office stood ajar, and he could glimpse Bane at his desk, the black sofa which had accorded him such a fine hiding place the night before, and the skeleton. The secretary smiled up into the Ranger's gray-green eyes.

"Good morning, sir. Dr. Bane is very busy now. He's feeling the death of Mr. Mallory, one of our most beloved patients. Mr. Mallory died of heart trouble in his sleep last night. The doctor's making out the death certificate and the funeral will be at four P.M. today. All of our patients are invited to attend."

"That's mighty nice," said Hatfield gravely. "I just dropped in on my way to the gate to tell the doc I'm headin' for town to send for more money. I got some put away in a savin's bank near where I used to work."

Bane heard their voices and glanced

up, frowning. His chair scraped, and the little man emerged from his office, to stare at Hatfield.

"Oh, yes — you're the cowboy with the stomach ache. What is it now?"

"Oh, I'm feelin' a mite better, Doc. Just a hair, that is, but enough to give me hope. I like it here and if it's all the same to you, I'm goin' to telegraph for some more money so's I can stick around a whole month."

"Glad that you like it, and are feeling better." Bane nodded suavely.

Bane wore pin-stripe trousers and fine, shining boots of soft leather, a frock coat and a white vest. Despite his small size he had a self-important manner and had learned, somewhere in his murky past, to imitate a physician's best bedside manner.

'The little devil, you'd never guess from lookin' at him, what he's up to behind that smooth front!' mused the Ranger.

Only about Bane's strange eyes, with the myriad lines radiating from the corners, was there sign of strain. There was his chief weakness — the violent, ungovernable temper which drove him to kill when he was opposed. Bane had a lot on is mind, thought Hatfield, as the Ranger played out his part of a simpleton completely absorbed in his own imaginary ailments.

Behind the curtain which hid Bane's black soul were terrible deeds and ambitions. There were the deaths of the Army doctor and Mallory, and the planned killings of Jay Rogers and Vance Thornton. Bane was maneuvering for an unassailable position, for control of the local government and destruction of witnesses who might try to pull him down.

'I'm as good as dead if he ever suspects me while he's got hold of me,' the Ranger told himself, as he smiled fatuously at the killer, Bane. 'He figgers he's close to real safety, and after a day or two, he won't have nothin' to worry about!'

It was an invisible seesaw, with

Bane at one end of the plank, the Ranger at the other. Physically, Hatfield outweighed Bane, but the psuedo doctor had collected a large and powerful strong-arm organization, through Frenchie DeLuys. Naturally such a connection would be vital to one of Bane's ambitions. Hatfield knew that Bane mentally was as keen as a razor edge, that his small enemy had a highly attuned sensitivity to danger where it concerned Bane's own safety, that Bane would never hesitate in striking an opponent down.

At the moment they were at a delicate point of balance. Hatfield had managed to capture Phelps, rescue Rogers, and shoot DeLuys, without the alarm reaching Bane. The seesaw was slowly coming down on his side, as he outbalanced Bane, but at the slightest hint of peril Bane might suddenly throw unsuspected weight into the game.

Bane was nodding, turning, his hands clasped behind his back as he returned to his den.

"I'll give you a pass," said the young lady at the desk, "so the attendants at the gate will let you by. Just a formality, you understand."

"Yes'm. I s'pose that's so nobody can run off without payin' the good doctor. He's a mighty fine feller, ain't he?"

"He is," she said, and smiled.

She believed it, too. She worked there, keeping records and interviewing patients, with no inkling of the real Bane. In his pose as a great physician he had fooled the public, and those who came to the Frontier Hospital, tricked by Phelps publicity.

Hatfield touched the brim of his Stetson and the young woman watched him, still smiling, as he stalked out and mounted the beautiful golden gelding. At the gates, the guards confronted him, but he showed the pass.

"I'll be back before long, fellers," he assured. "Yuh couldn't keep me out with a cannon, no sir! Just goin' after more cash. Doc Bane's treatin' me hisself. Says I got a mighty rare ailment." The Ranger spoke with pride.

"Shore, shore, cowboy. See yuh later." One guard grinned and winked at his companion.

The gate opened, and the Ranger rode through it, moving slowly along the dirt lane which ran into the road to Culverton.

"Bane's still mighty dangerous and I hope we're able to git to him before he smells a rat," he told the sorrel, as they picked up speed over the rise. "Frenchie's dead, but his gang's big and they got plenty gunnies to fight. I reckon Bane has thirty or forty fightin' hombres in the hospital grounds besides. They could hold off an army. And Bane's quarters is a reg'lar fort, with them barred winders and all."

Hatfield could get help now, through Thornton and Marshal Tate. He could get possemen to raid the enemy, but he did not desire to throw them against sure death. They might be cut to pieces before they could rush the barbed wire and the thick walls of the buildings.

"Got to figger on trickin' our way in," he growled. "And I'd shore hate to lose Bane! He could start it all over agin if he escapes."

17

Outlaw Den

ONE point kept troubling the Ranger, as he glanced back to make sure he was not followed or observed, and then turned into the main road from the long lane. He did not swing toward Culverton but west, heading into the wilds and rising hills.

'I wonder if Counselor Phelps is s'posed to be at Mallory's funeral this afternoon?' Bane would miss his confederate.

Of one thing Hatfield was certain. He would not charge the hospital barbed wire in daylight, for it would be too costly to the attackers, and might even result in the crushing of his allies.

'Bane buries 'em fast,' he mused. 'With an old feller like Mallory, who's got no close relations, no one would ever ask any questions.'

There was a small cemetery off on a hill not far from the hospital, and here it was that Bane would bury Mallory's remains. The Ranger had a great deal on his mind, as he sought to bring his forces to bear on the arch-enemy, Jonathan Bane.

Soon Hatfield had passed from the immediate vicinity of the hospital road. The highway was of reddish clay, rutted by the passing of an occasional farm wagon. His trained scout's eye told him that horsemen had come this way, in parties, not many hours before, and he grunted in satisfaction.

Goldy, rested from his stay in the coral, trotted briskly in the warm sunshine. A southerly breeze fanned them, and butterflies and bees hummed in the heat. Patches of woods and thick brush closed in. This was range country, but in the hills the foliage grew thick.

The Ranger was about two miles west of the turn-off to Bane's when he came on cattle sign. A small herd had been driven from the west and, he found, had been cut off the highway into the woods. He paused to investigate. It was, as he had thought, the bunch of steers which DeLuys' men had brought up the previous night, to the hospital pens. There was a small gap where they had been run into the brush, and the trail would lead to the creek hollow where Jason and his assistants could butcher them.

He returned to the road and kept riding, his alert eyes scanning the cattle sign. Three miles further along where the country was steep and the road petered out to a narrow trail, the cows had emerged from the woods.

Hatfield moved cautiously. He peered at the shadowed and sunlit wall of bush and saw an opening through which the rustlers had brought the cows. He rode past, watching, then turned the sorrel and came back. Gun in hand, he checked up before pushing into the monte.

His manner grew watchful. The trail winding through the wilderness was bordered by thick stands of trees and thorned bush. Any point might provide a spot for an ambush.

The sorrel walked slowly, ears pricked forward, sniffing at the air. Suddenly Goldy gave him warning. He scented man, just ahead at the turn.

Hatfield slipped from his saddle, Colt in hand, and pulled Goldy off the trail. He was taking only necessary precautions.

"All right, Ranger," a quiet voice called to him. "I'm here."

Marshal Zeke Tate emerged from the thicket at the turn, and approached.

"So yuh made it!" drawled Hatfield.

"Yeah. Easy enough with yore instructions and what yuh told us. Collected a posse and started before dawn. When we got past the hospital road, we took it slow till the light got good. Then it was simple to backtrack the cattle the outlaws had drove. We hid mighty careful, and about twenty riders, returnin' after deliverin' the cows to Bane's, went by and come in by this route. Thornton and the rest of the posse are hid up the way a bit. They been snoozin' to make up for lost sleep."

"*Bueno* — nice work, Marshal," complimented Hatfield. "There's been no alarm so far, that I savvy. Yuh got Phelps and the others safe and sound? And how'd Rogers seem when yuh left?"

"The boy come to about an hour after you rode off. He's weak from bein' beat up, but he ain't got no fatal hurts. Vance and me had to hustle to collect the boys before it got light."

"Yuh ain't tracked further than this, have yuh?"

"Nope. Figgered we'd better wait for you."

Vance Thornton, in leather pants and jacket to ward off thorns, guns belted at his heavy waist and a double-barreled shotgun in one hand, rose up to greet the tall Ranger, grinning.

233

"Mighty glad yuh're here, Jim. We're all set. Fetched fifty possemen along."

"We'll need 'em. Give orders for every man to keep his mouth shut. No unnecesary talkin' and each feller's responsible for his hoss. Muzzle 'em with bandannas, if need be. Now foller me."

The Ranger rode past the posse. Many of them were the same fellows who had accompanied Marshal Tate on the run to the KL, a citizen force recruited and sworn in according to law by the marshal.

They stared at the tall man, at the silver star on silver circle pined to his vest. He was a Texas Ranger, and they would follow him in the expected battle.

Hatfield scouted ahead. It was easy for him to follow the fresh sign made by the cows and the mounted outlaws. He was alert, ready for anything, but the wilderness remained undisturbed, with flitting birds and insects in the patches of sunlight, the low rustle of the brush in the warm breeze.

Now and then through vistas, he could see stretches of partially cleared rangeland on one side of him, but the other side was still dominated by brush. The trail branched and he swung the sorrel left, for the steers had come that way. The country dipped down, and the narrow valley made by a small stream was choked with wild timber and thorny growth.

When he reached the brook, he dismounted and inspected the soft earth along its banks. Cattle and horses had paused here to drink, and he let Goldy have a little water. He crossed the stream and the trail went up the other side, northward for a time.

It was about three-thirty by the sun when he emerged into a roughly made corral in the woods which covered the ravine and the steep slopes hemming it in. Here, obviously, DeLuys had held prime beefs which his men had stolen and held until time to drive another supply to Bane's.

Hatfield let Marshal Zeke Tate come up.

"We ain't far from the den now, Marshal," he said, his voice low. "I'm goin' to snake around and find the blind trail to their camp. Pass the word down the line to keep it quiet, savvy?"

The woods corral was empty, its collection of beefs having been run to the hospital the previous night.

Hatfield rode slowly around. There were several faint trails, but he chose one which was clearer and came in near the corral gate which was made of heavy lengths of tree trunks hewed from the forest. He dropped his reins, waved a warning hand to Tate and, afoot, started up the path he had picked.

It ended only a quarter of a mile further on, at the outlaw encampment. The first thing he heard was the stamping and restless sounds of a large number of horses. They were in a natural corral in the woods, bordering the stream. The bandits could not be far off, he thought, as he took to the woods and, keeping low, worked around so that the wind would be from the camp. Now he smelled wood smoke on the breeze, and heard faint noises of men.

The growth was thick, but he crept and crawled closer. At last, through a hole in the brush, he saw the shielded hollow in which the DeLuys' camp lay. Walls of the ravine which had been undercut in some ancient flood rose steeply. The shelves offered shelter from rain for men and equipment, and tarpaulins gave further protection. Saddles and other gear could be seen, and men were lounging around.

Some were broiling strips of beef on forked sticks at a wood fire, for in such a large gathering always a few were hungry. Others were napping, or drinking; card games went on here and there.

A couple of men with carbines were sitting on higher points. Evidently they were sentries, but there was no thought of danger or alarm, and the guards were not alert.

'About fifty to sixty of 'em in there!' Hatfield decided. 'DeLuys' recruited a bunch for Bane.'

What with the men working at the hospital, the enemy could muster around a hundred fighting men. It took money obtained by plenty of looting to maintain such a force, but Bane had flown high, wide and handsome, mused the Ranger.

Having smelled out the foe, he backed off and returned to warn Tate and Thornton.

The Ranger gave detailed orders as to the disposition of the posse, for he did not wish to lead them into a slaughter. DeLuys' outlaws were tough, and had proven that. They also were well-armed.

Marshal Tate set several men to take care of the mustangs, as Hatfield told him. Then the Ranger led one wing around, while Tate took the other file of dismounted, armed deputies. They would work into position until they surrounded the camp, and Hatfield would open the party.

The minutes seemed to crawl, fraught as they were with danger while they were moving up. But at last Hatfield reached the other side of the hollow. Tate's contingent did not have so far to travel, for the steep walls of the ravine would cut off escape that way.

One of the camp sentries was standing up, rifle in his hand, staring suspiciously at the south woods.

"What's up, Lew?" called a big outlaw who sported a thick black beard and seemed to be a leader. "See somethin'?"

"Thought I seen a shine of light on a gunbarrel," replied the guard.

"Watch out. Might be Frenchie and the boys comin'."

Hatfield edged in closer, his Winchester carbine loaded and ready, Colts waiting in their supple holsters. The deputies kept a good line, in spite of the underbrush. He signaled them to take cover and, leaping up, his stentorian voice filled the ravine:

"Throw down, outlaws! Yuh're surrounded!" And he added, "Surrender in the name of the Texas Rangers!"

"The Rangers!"

The cry stampeded the bandit camp. Men leaped from sleep, snatching up their guns. Tate and his column were coming through the trees, charging, with cowboy yells shrill in their throats.

The big fellow with the black whiskers was belowing commands as he opened fire with a sawed-off shotgun, spattering the bush. Hatfield picked him off with a well-placed carbine shot, and the big man threw up his hands and fell.

Crouched in the van, Hatfield sought out the gunny lieutenants, in command in DeLuys' absence. He could recognize them as they sought to rally their followers and get some order into the defense of the encampment. Tate's fire knocked over a sentry, and the lead sang thick in the warm air of the late afternoon.

"Put 'em away, boys!" shouted Hatfield, his powerful voice rising over the din of cursing outlaws and spitting guns.

Some ran away, hoping to reach the horses, and escape. Others fought on desperately, in snarling knots among the rocks. Tate was sweeping them up, and Hatfield pressed ever in.

"Throw down, outlaws!" he warned again. "Throw down or yuh'll be wiped out! Surrender to the Rangers!"

The blasting Colts' flamed; accurate, deadly. He had picked off three leaders, and the bandits were trapped, surrounded in their camp. Irresolutely one threw down his gun and raised his hands, squatting in the hope of not being hit. Two more saw him and followed suit, stunned by the fire and by the Rangers strategy.

Soon it was over, with the Ranger in control. The deputies closed in, driving prisoners taken in the woods before them. Outlaws with raised hands and frightened eyes, some bleeding from bullet wounds, stood in the clearing, Ranger captives.

"Clean up!" ordered the Ranger. "Clean up, boys. Herd 'em all against that rock wall and make shore none keeps any souvenirs like knives and Colts. Pronto, now."

The last rays of the sun to penetrate the ravine touched the silver star on silver circle — the emblem of the Rangers.

Tate's men were hastily obeying. Guns and other weapons were swept up while the owners were collected in a spot with the high rock behind them. Evil eyes, sullen and filled with hatred, stared at the Law.

When they had the captives properly secure, Hatfield called a council.

"We'll have a bite and a rest, boys, right here. We want to make Bane's after dark. So take it easy till the signal."

There was plenty of food and drink in the stores under the shelves of stone. Hatfield had some fried beef, hardtack, and hot beans from a big stone pot warming on a fire. He was resting on one arm, smoking after the meal, when one of Tate's deputies who had been down at the horse corral came hotfooting it in to report.

"Ranger — Marshall Tate — we caught a prisoner!"

"Fetch him in and let him join the collection," said Tate.

"This hombre's from the other direction," explained the deputy. "He come ridin' right into our hands from the out-trail."

"Let's have a peek at him," ordered Hatfield.

Soon they brought in the horseman, a heavy-set fellow with a round head and brown hair. He was angry, swearing at his captors.

"By gee, it's Jason, the butcher from Bane's!" exclaimed the Ranger, jumping to his feet.

"What's the idea of this?" demanded Jason furiously. "I'm a law-abidin' citizen and yuh got no right to arrest me! I was just out for a ride." He broke off as he stared at Hatfield's tall figure. "Huh? Say, I savvy you! You're from the hospital. Tell 'em who I am!" Now he saw the silver star on silver circle and evidently knew what it was. "Yuh — yuh, mean yuh're a Texas Ranger?" he went on, amazed.

Those around laughed. Hatfield nodded.

"That's me, Jason. I s'pose yuh come to see Frenchie? Well, he's kickin' up daisies, and as yuh can see, his gang's in a purty pickle. What you doin' here, so far off yore usual place?"

"Nothin', I tell yuh — just out a-ridin'," insisted Jason sullenly.

"Search him," ordered Hatfield.

"We already took two pistols and a knife off him," said a deputy.

Further careful search, and Hatfield opened the note which Jason carried in

244

an inside pocket. It was to Frenchie DeLuys and read:

DeLuys: Come at once, with every available man. Something is wrong. I'm not sure what yet, but am trying to find out. B.

"Bane's smelt a rat," growled Hatfield, to Tate and Thornton. "Mebbe he's missed Phelps. We'll have to get goin'. Saddle up, load yore guns, and we'll leave a few men here with the prisoners tied up till we can send for 'em. Hustle."

He was deeply troubled. Several things, any one of which might have warned the keenly attuned Bane, preyed on his mind. A slip, and Bane might elude him.

"They'll be on special watch at the gates," he thought, "if Bane's on the prod."

18

Arch-Enemy

EARLY dark had fallen, though the moon was still below the horizon, when Hatfield slowly approached the gates of the Frontier Hospital, He whistled cheerily, aware of the armed guards behind the thick wire, who peered out at him. The lanterns on the post cast a yellow glow over the scene.

Hatfield broke into song:

Oh, my gal's a lulu, every inch a lulu!

"Hi, you, what's all the joy for?" sang out a guard, coming hastily to the gate.

"Hullo, fellers, how's ev'rything? I jush lef' best s'loon in Texas down below. 'Oh, my gal's a lulu — '"

"Dry up, yuh big fool," said the sentry. "Yuh'll disturb the whole hospital."

Now he recognized the patient, Hart, who had gone out early in the day. Obviously the patient had been imbibing at one of the town hostelries.

"Let me in," said Hatfield, at the gate. "Doc Banes says I'm mighty interestin'. Got a stummick like a rusted boiler. Open up!"

"All right, but keep it quiet. Yuh better get to bed before yuh land in trouble."

The sentry unlocked the gates, and swung one back so the sorrel could enter, with Hatfield swaying on his back.

There were three more sentries on the gate — twice as many as usual — and Hatfield was aware there were bunches of armed men near Bane's office, on the porch, watching. The guards grinned at the spectacle of the drunken cowboy coming in from town.

They leaned on their shotguns.

The drum of hoofs sounded on the lane, approaching, and the guards grew quickly alert. A horseman with his bandanna drawn up as a mask, and slouching his saddle, rode up rapidly.

"Frenchie's comin' — whole bunch of the boys with him," reported the messenger.

It was one of Tate's deputies, fixed up as a bandit. His gruff voice was good enough to fool the sentries for the necessary space of time. Hatfield turned Goldy. The gate guards had forgotten him as they peered out at the large band of riders rushing in.

Again Hatfield's strategy proved successful. The fake message, the drawn masks in the night, tricked the sentries. The gateman failed to lock the gate and the horsemen came sweeping in.

Hey, there, where's DeLuys? Take it easy!" The captain of the gate sang out wildly as he had to jump aside to keep from being run down by heavy mustangs.

"This ain't Frenchie's bunch!" shrieked another sentry.

Their guns rose. Hatfield, with Colts up, winged the captain as the man tried to fire into the bunched deputies. Tate and Thornton urged their men inside the enclosure.

Blasting muzzles spat led and fire. Hoarse shouts came from the reserves who were waiting at the main building. But the pose and the Ranger were inside the enclosure. They spread out, riding hard, low over their horses, elusive targets in the night.

The demoralized defense forces broke and ran as the heavy firing blasted them back. Some took cover behind building corners, but Hatfield and Tate, Thornton and the rest circled, drove them out into the waiting arms of possemen. One after another, Bane's men were captured or run into hiding places about the ground.

"Done it agin!" crowed Zeke Tate triumphantly, as he rejoined the Texas Ranger. "The hospital's our'n, Hatfield."

"C'mon! I've got to locate Bane."

The Ranger made the front porch, and leaped from saddle. Colt in hand, he tried the front door. It was unlocked. He went in, wary as a hunting panther, and through to Bane's office. A lamp, turned down low, was on the desk, but though he looked everywhere, even behind the horsehair sofa, he could not find Bane.

Tate and the Ranger, with plenty of men to back them, spread through the house. They roused startled servants, and patients in the other wings, but Bane was not there.

After an exhaustive hunt, the Ranger had to admit his quarry had eluded him.

"Cuss Bane!" he growled. "He's slipped the noose somehow! Smelt trouble and has took it on the run!"

"We cleaned up his whole gang, though," said Thornton.

"Bane can recruit new ones easy enough," said the Ranger anxiously.

"I got to find him!"

He would not rest, with Bane free.

★ ★ ★

"Stafford — Stafford!" shouted the conductor, as the train drew up for a brief moment at the signal stop on the railroad.

Hatfield, hidden inside the freight shed, peered up the line.

"There he goes, hoppin' on the train!" he muttered.

He watched the small, quick-moving man board the train, a carpet-bag in one hand. Then Hatfield hurried out and caught the last step-rail, swinging aboard. He started up through the cars, and men and women stared at the tall, grim figure of the mighty Ranger on the prowl.

He had ridden full-tilt from Bane's place to Culverton, but Bane had not showed there. Hatfield had rushed on, sure that his quarry would seek quick escape, somehow warned of his peril.

And now he had reached the end of the long trail.

Hatfield stepped across the gap between the creaking cars as the train picked up speed. He glanced through the open door, and there was Bane, about to drop into a vacant seat halfway up the car. Bane looked all around, carefully, and caught the Ranger's gray-green, icy eyes.

He left his seat with a catlike bound, a gun flashing into his hand. The face was livid with his fury and hate for the tall man who had tracked him down. About his eyes the lines had deepened, the skin whitening as it tautened.

The car jerked, rattling as the wheels crossed some points. Bane had pulled his trigger, and the Ranger heard the whirl of the lead and a dull thud as the bullet hit the partition close by. The Ranger Colt must be accurate. There were women and children and other innocent people in the railway car.

Screams rent the air, with the heavy explosion of the Ranger gun. Hatfield felt the kick of his pistol against his hand. Bane staggered, caught at the arm of a seat, and rolled slowly over in a heap.

Hatfield hurried to check up. Bane was dead, a bluish hole between the fading, once fierce eyes. The carpetbag was crammed with metal and paper money, Bane's available loot.

* * *

"And that's it, Cap'n McDowell," said Hatfield, as he made his brief report at Austin headquarters. "This Bane was the leadin' spirit, cheatin' sick folks and those who thought they was sick. He had a bad record, and he killed that Army major to protect hisself. Killed others as he went along, to gain power. One of his aides, Frenchie DeLuys, drygulched Horace Youngs, so's Bane could grab Youngs' place cheap, to use as his headquarters.

"Bane poisoned an old miner named Mallory to get his money. I found out

253

a lot for myself, and what else I needed to know was told me by Sam Phelps, who was Bane's chief helper down there. Jay Rogers, the reporter, aims to marry Della Thornton, and he's goin' to run the Culverton *Call* like a real Frontier paper should be run. Marshal Tate and Vance Thornton are seein' to them captured outlaws, and to Phelps.

"That last day, Bane got leery. He missed Phelps, and took a run to town after I'd left the hospital, to try and find Phelps. When he couldn't he sent a message to DeLuys, but hid hisself outside the hospital grounds till he saw what happened. I figgered out that Bane had run for the railroad, and managed to come up with him. He refused to surrender and I had to shoot him."

"Good riddance," grunted McDowell, eyes glowing. "I wish I'd been there for the party." McDowell was proud of Hatfield, of his officer's prowess and efficiency. "Yuh done a great job, Ranger."

McDowell cleared his throat, frowning as he rattled a sheaf of reports on his desk.

"Well," asked Hatfield softly, "where's the fuss now, Cap'n?"

"It's a big one, down on the Border. But you just got in from Culverton and yuh're tired."

"I'll be ready in a jiffy," said Hatfield rising.

It wasn't long before Captain Bil McDowell was watching the tall Ranger on the golden sorrel wave farewell. Hatfield swung off, carrying Lone Star Law to the far reaches of the mighty state.

TOP HAND
Wade Everett

The Broken T was big. But no ranch is big enough to let a man hide from himself.

GUN WOLVES OF LOBO BASIN
Lee Floren

The Feud was a blood debt. When Smoke Talbot found the outlaws who gunned down his folks he aimed to nail their hide to the barn door.

SHOTGUN SHARKEY
Marshall Grover

The westbound coach carrying the indomitable Larry and Stretch headed for a shooting showdown.

FIGHTING RAMROD
Charles N. Heckelmann

Most men would have cut their losses, but Frazer counted the bullets in his guns and said he'd soak the range in blood before he'd give up another inch of what was his.

LONE GUN
Eric Allen

Smoke Blackbird had been away too long. The Lequires had seized the Blackbird farm, forcing the Indians and settlers off, and no one seemed willing to fight! He had to fight alone.

THE THIRD RIDER
Barry Cord

Mel Rawlins wasn't going to let anything stand in his way. His father was murdered, his two brothers gone. Now Mel rode for vengeance.

ARIZONA DRIFTERS
W. C. Tuttle

When drifting Dutton and Lonnie Steelman decide to become partners they find that they have a common enemy in the formidable Thurston brothers.

TOMBSTONE
Matt Braun

Wells Fargo paid Luke Starbuck to outgun the silver-thieving stagecoach gang at Tombstone. Before long Luke can see the only thing bearing fruit in this eldorado will be the gallows tree.

HIGH BORDER RIDERS
Lee Floren

Buckshot McKee and Tortilla Joe cut the trail of a border tough who was running Mexican beef into Texas. They stopped the smuggler in his tracks.

BRETT RANDALL, GAMBLER
E. B. Mann

Larry Day had the choice of running away from the law or of assuming a dead man's place. No matter what he decided he was bound to end up dead.

THE GUNSHARP
William R. Cox

The Eggerleys weren't very smart. They trained their sights on Will Carney and Arizona's biggest blood bath began.

THE DEPUTY OF SAN RIANO
Lawrence A. Keating and
Al. P. Nelson

When a man fell dead from his horse, Ed Grant was spotted riding away from the scene. The deputy sheriff rode out after him and came up against everything from gunfire to dynamite.

FARGO: MASSACRE RIVER
John Benteen

The ambushers up ahead had now blocked the road. Fargo's convoy was a jumble, a perfect target for the insurgents' weapons!

SUNDANCE: DEATH IN THE LAVA
John Benteen

The Modoc's captured the wagon train and its cargo of gold. But now the halfbreed they called Sundance was going after it . . .

HARSH RECKONING
Phil Ketchum

Five years of keeping himself alive in a brutal prison had made Brand tough and careless about who he gunned down . . .

FARGO: PANAMA GOLD
John Benteen

With foreign money behind him, Buckner was going to destroy the Panama Canal before it could be completed. Fargo's job was to stop Buckner.

FARGO:
THE SHARPSHOOTERS
John Benteen

The Canfield clan, thirty strong were raising hell in Texas. Fargo was tough enough to hold his own against the whole clan.

PISTOL LAW
Paul Evan Lehman

Lance Jones came back to Mustang for just one thing — revenge! Revenge on the people who had him thrown in jail.

HELL RIDERS
Steve Mensing

Wade Walker's kid brother, Duane, was locked up in the Silver City jail facing a rope at dawn. Wade was a ruthless outlaw, but he was smart, and he had vowed to have his brother out of jail before morning!

DESERT OF THE DAMNED
Nelson Nye

The law was after him for the murder of a marshal — a murder he didn't commit. Breen was after him for revenge — and Breen wouldn't stop at anything . . . blackmail, a frameup . . . or murder.

DAY OF THE COMANCHEROS
Steven C. Lawrence

Their very name struck terror into men's hearts — the Comancheros, a savage army of cutthroats who swept across Texas, leaving behind a bloodstained trail of robbery and murder.

SUNDANCE: SILENT ENEMY
John Benteen

A lone crazed Cheyenne was on a personal war path. They needed to pit one man against one crazed Indian. That man was Sundance.

LASSITER
Jack Slade

Lassiter wasn't the kind of man to listen to reason. Cross him once and he'll hold a grudge for years to come — if he let you live that long.

LAST STAGE TO GOMORRAH
Barry Cord

Jeff Carter, tough ex-riverboat gambler, now had himself a horse ranch that kept him free from gunfights and card games. Until Sturvesant of Wells Fargo showed up.

McALLISTER ON THE COMANCHE CROSSING
Matt Chisholm

The Comanche, McAllister owes them a life — and the trail is soaked with the blood of the men who had tried to outrun them before.

QUICK-TRIGGER COUNTRY
Clem Colt

Turkey Red hooked up with Curly Bill Graham's outlaw crew. But wholesale murder was out of Turk's line, so when range war flared he bucked the whole border gang alone . . .

CAMPAIGNING
Jim Miller

Ambushed on the Santa Fe trail, Sean Callahan is saved by two Indian strangers. But there'll be more lead and arrows flying before the band join Kit Carson against the Comanches.

GUNSLINGER'S RANGE
Jackson Cole

Three escaped convicts are out for revenge. They won't rest until they put a bullet through the head of the dirty snake who locked them behind bars.

RUSTLER'S TRAIL
Lee Floren

Jim Carlin knew he would have to stand up and fight because he had staked his claim right in the middle of Big Ike Outland's best grass.

THE TRUTH ABOUT SNAKE RIDGE
Marshall Grover

The troubleshooters came to San Cristobal to help the needy. For Larry and Stretch the turmoil began with a brawl and then an ambush.

...NGE

...at nothing,
...d him first
...te Manly's

gun. the dirty snake who locked ...
behind bars.

DEVIL'S DINERO
Marshall Grover

Pl... ...old
...le-
...in
...ns.

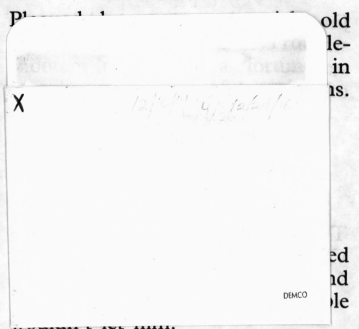

...ed
...d
...le